Sweet Lady

By

Elaine Spires

Sweet Lady by Elaine Spires ISBN: 978-1-291-15678-2

Copyright © Elaine Spires 2012

In loving memory of Lily Spires

And with grateful thanks to Vikki Ingram and Myron McKay who first believed in this story.

Author's Note

Sweet Lady started life as a short play that I wrote and produced at the Anna Scher Theatre, London. I then reworked it into a three act play and it was first performed as such in St John's, Antigua, with myself, Vikki Ingram and Myron McKay playing the three main roles. It has always been a story I've been fond of and I'm please to present it to you now as a novel, which I sincerely hope you will enjoy.

I would also like to thank Lisa Moreno at Vanilla Gecko for the design of the cover.

And my increasing band of loyal readers for all their support, especially after the furore of Singles' Holiday. May you enjoy Sweet Lady as much!

Please visit my website www.elainespires.co.uk

Chapter One

How had it come to this? How had we come to be here; nervous and on edge, sitting in *an atmosphere,* in silence, neither of us wanting to discuss it or even talk to each other? The only sound in the hot, stuffy room that morning was from the large, old-fashioned grandfather clock that marked each passing second with a loud tick and whose face declared that in spite of it feeling like the longest morning of my life, it was really only ten past nine. I let my gaze wander around, taking in the cream walls with their sepia prints of a long-ago London, the deep, comfortable, tan leather chairs, the magnificent display of silk flowers standing on top of the antique chest of drawers over by the window, and felt cocooned from the rest of the world just by being here inside this plush, elegant room where everything was conducive to making you feel secure and relaxed. Outside this cosy womb, much of the world was getting ready to celebrate and to rejoice; preparing to sit, glued to its television sets, drinking, eating and watching every detail of the marriage of Prince William to Kate Middleton later that morning. I'd watched some of the news coverage earlier; I'd been awake for hours by then; my whole night had been spent tossing and turning and going over scenes in my head and imagining what this morning would bring, thinking of how many different ways Eleanor might play up or cause an unnecessary fuss, while the Prince married the Commoner a couple of miles, yet a million light-years, away. I jumped suddenly, startled by the sound of the air conditioning unit jolting into life.

"Thank God for that!" Eleanor said as she continued to leaf through a copy of Conde Nast in the chair next to me. "I thought they were going to leave us to roast to death."

I managed a shadow of a smile at my mother's comment knowing that none of my own was needed or expected. She looked as far from roasting to death as was humanly possible. I was always the one with sweat running down her head, her clothes wet and stuck to her and a bright red face, while she could be in thirty-six degrees and ninety percent humidity and look like cool perfection. I knew my mother well; I recognised the signs that she was as wound up this morning as a tightly-coiled spring; her right foot swinging up and down betrayed her impatience. After a couple more moments of frantic page turning she threw the magazine down on the low table in front of us and looked at her watch for the fifth time in as many minutes, tossing her hair that still bore the honey-blonde streaks that a winter in the sun had put there as she did so. I wondered why, when there was such an obvious timepiece in the room in the shape of the grandfather clock, that Eleanor found the need to keep checking her watch. I was glad she did, though, because while she was doing other things she wasn't talking; wasn't launching into the tirade that was bubbling just below the surface and which I knew was going to erupt as sure as I knew that night follows day. And I didn't have to wait very long; within seconds it began.

"God! I hate these places," Eleanor said, her enormous dark eyes looking round the room, then standing up straightening out imaginary creases in her grey and pink outfit.

"Places? How many places like this have you been in before then?" I said, mentally kicking my own shins because I knew she would rise to the bait but I was completely unable to stop myself.

"Don't be clever, Victoria! I mean clinics and hospitals in general."

"I've never been anywhere that looked less like a hospital," I retorted.

"That's exactly my point!" she snapped back. "There's always an atmosphere, isn't there? Even if it doesn't look like a hospital, you're still fully aware that you're in one. I mean, if someone blindfolded you and brought you inside a hospital you'd know immediately where you were, wouldn't you?" She looked around the room again and shuddered. "I hate being surrounded by sick people!"

I turned my head slowly to look at my mother then shook it in disbelief. Sometimes she really was something else.

"You're not surrounded by sick people, are you? We're in the waiting room of an exclusive private clinic. Where are all the sick people here?" I asked, looking around the room slowly in an exaggerated way. "I can't see any."

Eleanor tutted and gave me a filthy look, an expression of distain on her face.

"Don't split hairs! You know what I mean," she said. It never occurred to her that I might not. She looked at her watch again. "And what is it with always keeping you waiting? Eh? Why do you never go in on time? Is there some rule written somewhere that you have to be kept waiting?"

I shrugged and looked at my feet. She was usually a kind, loving, fun person, but when she liked she could be a real cow. Nobody wanted today to be over more than I did, but I thought it best to say nothing in case I brought more of her wrath down on my head. However, my mother was on a roll and she was nowhere near finished.

"I mean, why bother to give you an appointment time if it's going to be ignored? Why send you an itinerary for the morning when they know they're going to keep you sitting in the bloody waiting room?"

"They're probably busy. Perhaps they've had an emergency or something. We aren't the only people here. As you say, it's a hospital, so anything could have happened."

"Well, it's hardly a busy A and E Department, is it? It's a private clinic. No, they do it on purpose."

"You're paranoid!"

"I'm not! It's as if they're putting you in your place, you know, they're telling you that they're doing you a favour by seeing you. Especially in a case like this. They're letting you know that you don't really matter; they're the important ones and you're well and truly in their hands so they call all the shots. You're not important, you're just the patient."

I gave an inward sigh. I'd known that this was going to happen. I'd known that Eleanor would find fault with everything and everyone this morning. She was a celebrity; people jumped at her every whim and danced attendance on her so she was used to getting her own way. And on the rare occasions that she didn't get instant gratification she'd complain and cause a fuss. Usually it worked; today, it didn't.

"We were early," I pointed out. "The appointment's half nine and it's only twenty past now. I told you we left too early. I told you it wouldn't take us that long to get here."

8

"Well, it's better to be too early than too late. You never know what the traffic's going to be like at this time of the morning, especially today of all days with people rushing to the supermarket to top up on booze and food to sit at home and watch the wedding. And anyway, what was the point in hanging around at home if we were ready? It's best to be up and out when you've got things to do. *Carpe diem* as they say."

Things to do? Well, that was one way of putting it.

I picked up a magazine that Eleanor had put down earlier and started to look through it at the exquisitely decorated homes with tables covered in rich fare and models wearing glamorous, glitzy outfits. It was a Christmas edition of a French magazine. She stood up again and wandered around the room looking at the old photos in an abstracted way, not really taking in what she saw. She suddenly stopped and sniffed deeply.

"There's always a smell, too," she said, sniffing again and refusing to let it drop. "It's a mixture of disinfectant, anaesthetic and ... wee."

"For God's sake, Mum! This is a private clinic. It's five hundred pounds a night just for the bed. It does not smell of wee!"

"I don't need any reminding of the price, Victoria! I'm the one who's footing the bill, remember!" she snapped, turning round sharply to face me. She always gets prickly if I call her 'Mum' and not 'Eleanor' but my retort about money had provided just the opening she had been waiting for. I threw the magazine down on the table in disgust and exasperation. God knows, I loved my mother; I loved her with all my heart and soul. I was the image of her physically. *'You look like two of those Russian dolls that fit inside each other,'* someone had once said to us. But our characters were very different. And sometimes I could easily murder her.

"Oh, here we go! I knew you'd start! I just knew that sooner or later your money would come into the conversation."

Eleanor strode back across the room and sat down next to me, her beautiful face transformed into an angry snarl.

"He didn't even *offer* to pay."

"He has no money."

"Ha! Don't make me laugh! He could have got the money from somewhere if he'd wanted to. He always seems to have enough to keep himself in weed and beers. He could have at least offered, shown willing."

My face flushed and I could feel my anger rising. Why was my mother always so bloody unfair about some things? She was a highly intelligent woman, so why did she seem to relish being so unreasonable sometimes? Why did she seem to enjoy digging the knife in? Why did she so love being a bitch? Today she was being a drama queen and a real diva.

"What do you mean *'He should offer and show willing'*? Why? To give you the chance to laugh in his face? He has his pride, Mum."

"Pride? Pride's never stopped him taking money before, has it? Where was his pride when he was working the beaches fleecing tourists? Where was his pride in coming here on an open-ended free holiday? Eh? He hasn't had to foot the bill for anything at all, not in Antigua and not since he's been here. All along he's been more than happy to take, take, take! And how can you even suggest I'd laugh in his face? How can you say such a thing? I wouldn't have done that.

You know I wouldn't have laughed at him. He was probably afraid that if he offered to shell out that I'd take him up on it."

"Mum, he's not working so where is he supposed to get money from? Eh? You know there's no way that he could afford to pay the bill here. You know it and he knows it. So what's the point of offering something he can't do? That would have just given you the chance to have yet another go at him. Why go through the charade?"

"Have another go at him?" Her voice had gone up half an octave. "Me? When have I had a go at him?"

"Oh, Mum! You're always on at him, all the time. You have a go at any opportunity. He can't do right for doing wrong as far as you're concerned, especially for the last few days. All you've done is criticise him and find fault with him. You've got an honours degree in putting him down. It's like you get a huge kick out of it."

"Don't be ridiculous! You don't know what you're talking about! I admit I'm critical of the fact that he doesn't seem to have ever been able to hold down a proper job, but I don't keep on putting him down as you seem to be accusing me of. It's just the assumption that I'd pick up the bill that gets me. He just assumed it would be me. He's never once even discussed who might be paying for all this." She waved her hand to indicate the room. "He's never even broached the subject. Never even asked how much the whole thing may be costing."

"Right! Okay! Whatever you say!" I retorted, turning sideways in my chair so that my back was to her. When she was like this there was no reasoning with her.

We both sat in an angry silence for a few moments then Eleanor opened her handbag and took out her cigarettes, diving back into the bag looking for her lighter. Realising what she was doing, I turned back towards her and simply stared.

"Eleanor, you can't smoke in here."

She looked at me and then took a long, slow, exaggerated look around the room.

"There's no sign," she said, flicking her lighter and drawing deeply on the cigarette. I waved my hand in front of my face furiously in an attempt to remove the smoke, desperately hoping she wouldn't set off the smoke alarm. She was really starting to wind me up.

"This is a hospital! You can't smoke in a hospital! You can't smoke anywhere inside a building, yet alone a hospital! It's against the law as you well know! Even for people like you," I added, nastily. Now I was the one on a roll. "Just stop being so bloody childish! What if you set off the smoke alarm? Do you think that's clever? Do you?"

She ignored me.

"I don't believe you sometimes. If you don't care about your own health think about mine," I said, waving the smoke away again. "Or think about the baby's!"

Eleanor dropped her cigarette on the tiled floor, narrowly avoiding the silk rug and made much of putting it out with her slim, elegant foot. She then dived into her handbag again for a tissue, which she used to pick it up and then drop it in the bin at the far side of the room, admonishing me as she went.

"This is an abortion clinic, Victoria; a baby's welfare doesn't come high on the agenda here, does it?"

I winced at her insensitivity, but Eleanor hadn't finished. "Anyway, how many times do I have to tell you? It's not a baby. It's not even a proper foetus at this stage. It's just a bunch of cells."

I'd had enough. I leapt from the chair, my face inches away from my mother's, crimson with rage. "Stop it! How can you talk like that? That's a horrible thing to say, even for you!"

"But it's the truth. Why should the truth be so horrible?"

"There's no reasoning with you lately. Ever since the test result you've done nothing but bitch and moan. And you keep on taking it out on Tyrone and it's not his fault."

"Whose fault is it then?"

"It takes two to tango, Mum. Two. Not just Tyrone."

"Yes, well, perhaps he should have sat out at the last waltz." She crossed the room and plonked herself on an upright, upholstered chair. I knew what would be coming next and started the count-down in my head.

"And where is he? Eh?" Eleanor said, staring defiantly at me, as if I was keeping this classified information from her. "Where is he?" Her trump card; he wasn't there with us.

"I don't know! But he'll be here, won't he?"

"Oh, yes, he'll be here all right; he'll be here when it's all over."

"But you heard him! He said he had a couple of things to do, calls to make, didn't he? He said he'd see us here. Here at half past nine."

But Eleanor wasn't listening; she was off on another roll.

"It was too much to expect he'd get here on time on such an important occasion to offer a bit of support, I suppose. He's selfish and self-centred. Everything is always about him!" She, the Sometime Queen of Self-Interest, said this with a straight face.

"He could be stuck in traffic, Mum. You said yourself that traffic can be bad at this time of the morning," I said, wondering why I was bothering to placate my mother or even to defend Tyrone, who had also done his fair share of winding me up over the last couple of months and really didn't deserve any kind of defence at all from me.

"Well, we sailed through, didn't we? The traffic didn't stop us getting here on time, did it? We were early in fact," Eleanor retorted, triumphantly. "And anyway, he's coming on the tube. No hold ups or delays today or we'd have heard about it on the radio. '*A good service on all underground lines*' is what they said earlier when we were in the car."

"Look! He said he'd be here and he will. He's not even late yet," I added, looking at the grandfather clock for confirmation, which fortunately now showed twenty-nine minutes past nine.

"Well, he's cutting it rather fine, isn't he?"

"There could be a million reasons why he's late."

"Yes, there could be. But there won't. You know as well as I do that there won't be."

"Just shut up, will you!" I said, throwing myself down on one of the leather chairs again, avoiding her eye, a wave of nausea rising. Eleanor was furious and she let it show.

"Don't speak to me like that! Don't you dare defend him! Why do you always defend him?"

"Why do you always slag him off?" I said quietly, lifting my gaze to meet hers this time. "Just give him a chance, for God's sake. If you kill somebody you get the chance to defend yourself. He's not even late yet so just back off, Mum! And even if he gets here a few minutes late, it's not the end of the world, is it?"

Eleanor shrugged. I softened my tone a degree or two.

"Perhaps he's gone to see those old mates of his, in Rainham. Or just wanted to be around his own people for a while…"

She shrugged again

"He might have gone to a job interview or something, you know, as a surprise, without telling us," I said, knowing I really was clutching at straws and pissed off with myself again for carrying the argument on.

"Don't make me laugh! A job interview!" Eleanor shrieked. "What work could he do? Especially here! He's a waster with no ambition. He's happy to just drift along. What can he put on his CV? Eh? *Previous experience? Bumming a living from tourists.* Employers will hardly be beating a path to his door, will they? Making a bit here and there from selling weed and poncing off women is all he wants out of life. There's more chance of striking oil under Tower Bridge than there is of him getting a job, or even looking for one. And anyway, I thought it was all agreed and made clear that he's going back to Antigua soon. After all this, I think even he might be sensitive enough to feel that he could have outstayed his welcome."

"Do you know something, Mum?" I said, standing up and clutching my fists as I felt myself boiling up. "You talk about Tyrone in exactly the same way that you used to talk about my dad. Exactly the same attitude. Exactly the same tone. And do you know what?"

"No. Go on. Surprise me with a gem of witty observation," she said, looking at me in her amused, sarcastic way.

"I think you're still bitter about my dad running out on you when you told him you were pregnant with me. And you're taking out all the pent-up anger you feel at him on Tyrone. And it's not fair. You're not even giving him a chance!"

I flopped down onto the chair again; it was as if the speech had exhausted me; drained me. I was sick of fighting against her. Eleanor looked at me, shook her head and smiled.

"Oh, please! Spare me the amateur psychology, Victoria," she said.

The door sprang open and we both jumped. Tyrone stood in the doorway, his frame, tallish and muscular from his regular gym workouts, filling up most of it. He strutted into the room, his ponytail of braids swinging, his shades on his forehead, his jeans really low on his snake-hips, designer trainers on his feet and his Blackberry in his hand. He looked as if he didn't have a care in the world. He winked at me, patting my shoulder, as he took a seat across from the two of us.

"Waa gwan?" he said.

The words *red rag* and *bull* sprang to mind and Eleanor immediately rose to the challenge.

"Well! What a lovely surprise! Look who's here! What's happened, Tyrone? Nowhere else to go this morning so you thought you might join us?"

Tyrone leaned back on the chair and stretched his feet out in front of him and then turned to look at Eleanor.

"Mi promis fi ya. Mi waan ya. Mi ya."

"If you've got something to say speak so that we can understand you, for God's sake!"

When he wanted to, Tyrone spoke clear, articulate English with an educated-London accent. And then he could speak lazy Estuary English as well; after all he'd lived in Rainham in Essex with his dad for seven years and gone to school there. But he knew that speaking in Antiguan dialect was a sure way to wind Eleanor up. He leaned forward and now spoke slowly, exaggerating every word.

"I said. *'I said I'd be here. I want to be here. I'm here'*" he said.

Still Eleanor couldn't let it drop; she was itching for a fight.

"Yes, you are finally here. Late!"

"Sorry mi late."

"Mum! He's not late! We were early..." I was trying my best to calm things down. Tyrone looked across at me, his huge dark, almond eyes trying to reassure me; trying to tell me that he didn't want to cause any trouble today, but where Eleanor was concerned, well, it seemed to amuse him and he just couldn't help himself, either.

"It's okay, Vic," he said, raising his eyebrows. "Mi expec she fi kikup."

"Will you please speak in proper English?" Eleanor screeched at him.

"Please, Tyrone..." I said, feeling ill. This wasn't the time or place for the two of them to bait each other.

"Okay! Okay!" He sat back again in the chair, making himself comfortable and suddenly became serious. "Look, the reason I'm a little late is because... well, I've been talking things over with Mommy." He raised his Blackberry in the air and wiggled it back and forth in his hand.

Eleanor's look was one of pure venom. My heart sank and my stomach churned. Why was he doing this? Why was he deliberately winding her up? I hardly recognised her beautiful face as she screwed up her eyes, pushed her fair hair away and, barring her teeth seemed to give a snarl.

"What did you tell her for? It has nothing whatsoever to do with your mother!"

"She is the grandmother..." I heard a voice say and then realised it was me. "So she does have the right to a say."

"To interfere, you mean!" she was beside herself with anger.

"What have you got against Mommy? What's she ever done to you?" Tyrone asked Eleanor in genuine amazement.

"Apart from giving birth to you, do you mean?" she spat back at him.

I winced.

"So, come on! Give us all a laugh; what's Mommy's evangelical opinion on this situation that's really none of her business?"

"Eleanor! Stop it!" I shouted.

Seeing that I was upset seemed to affect Tyrone. He came and stood by me and put his hand on my shoulder and when he spoke again it was in a quieter, more reasonable way.

"Look, Eleanor, it's just like Vic says," he said, giving my shoulder another gentle squeeze. We were two tiny St Georges facing the might of the Dragon together. "Mommy's the baby's grandma. I'm the baby's daddy and that means we both got the right to a say in this, whether you like it or not." He sat on the chair next to me and was silent for a beat before he continued.

"Mi bin a tink bout dis."

He gave a half-smile of apology for his language lapse, quickly slapping his hand over his mouth in a gesture that was too late, and then he continued in English. "I've been awake all night thinking it over and over, and I don't want the abortion to go ahead. And Mommy agrees with me."

"I don't believe you!"

"Why didn't you say something before, Tyrone?" I asked. "Why have you left it until now?"

"I have never agreed with abortion. I think it's wrong. I think that whatever way you look at it, it's murder."

"That's not fair!" I interrupted him.

"Just let me have my say, Vic! I don't go along with all that 'a woman's got the right to do what she wants with her body' crap. I mean... she has, of course she has, to an extent," he added quickly when he saw our reaction to his words, "but a father's got rights, too. His opinion should carry some weight. Especially, as in this case, if he wants a child." He paused and looked at both of us as we stared at him, stunned by what he'd just said. "And, perhaps, if a woman don't want a kid then she should take precautions to make sure she don't get pregnant in the first place."

Eleanor leapt across the room. I stood up, afraid of what she might do. Even Tyrone seemed to shrink back in the chair a little.

"How dare you!" she roared.

Tyrone twitched; I could see he was dying for a smoke. But I could tell that he wasn't going to back down. He stood up and turning his back on her, wandered over to the window and leaned insolently against the chest of drawers.

"But, if she does get pregnant, okay, well, accidents happen. But I believe that if an accident happens, then it's all for a reason, you know what I'm saying? I think it's God's will. And I don't think the abortion should go ahead. It's wrong. It's wrong."

"Is that what Mommy's preacher tells her every Sunday?"

"Our Church does tell us to save life and not take it, yes. What could be wrong with that? Every child is a gift."

"Wait a minute! You're not suggesting you and your mother bring this child up, are you?" Eleanor asked him, incredulous.

"Well, why not?" He looked genuinely puzzled again.

"I'd have thought that was obvious!"

"Mommy's raised four kids on her own."

"You're hardly an advertisement for her parenting skills."

"Mommy did the best she could in hard circumstances. Very hard circumstances. Just like you did when you was raising Vic. But four times harder. You've no idea what she went through when we was kids. Nobody's better than her at raising pickneys. Mommy and me'll take care of it. My kid won't want for nuttin'."

Eleanor was so taken back by what he said, she sat down. My heart was racing. I hadn't seen this coming; couldn't have imagined in a million years that he'd feel this way.

"And you know what? I might surprise you," he continued. "I might just do a good job and make a really great daddy."

"You?" Eleanor sprung back up from the chair. "You can't even get yourself out of bed before noon. You've never even had a proper job! What would you be like waking up three, four, five times a night to change it or feed it? The child would starve to death! You spend most of your time stoned. Or are you planning on taking it up and down the beaches with you while you're pushing weed on tourists?"

Tyrone sucked his teeth and looked at her through half-shut eyes.

"Did you know what kind of mother you were going to be when you got pregnant with Vic?"

"No. No, I didn't" she admitted. "But I did have a sense of responsibility."

"Look, okay. I'm the first to say that I ain't shown much sense of responsibility til now. I've been a lot of things and I've done a lot of things that I ain't proud of. But I can be there for this kid. I can make something of my life now and I can give him something I never had and that's a daddy that stuck around. This kid's been sent for a reason. I just feel it."

"It's the Almighty's way of saving you? Is that what you mean? He's sending a child on the off chance of turning you into a decent human being? Don't be so ridiculous!"

Tyrone stood up and growled with frustration. I could feel the irritation coming from him in waves. He turned to Eleanor again.

"Why is it ridiculous to want to accept your responsibilities? I'm not taking the easy way out. I thought you'd approve of that. After all, you've given me enough shit in the last few days."

"You should have said something before this, Tyrone!" I said. They both turned and stared at me as if they'd forgotten I was in the room. Eleanor recovered first, shrugging as she spoke; dismissing me and my input.

"It doesn't matter whether he'd said something last week or yesterday. What he's saying now is totally ridiculous. Who in their right mind would hand a baby over to him? Or his mother?"

"I'm serious," he said, crossing to stand in front of her and prodding her with his finger as he spoke. "It's my child's life we're talking about here. I want to be responsible for my child. Abortion is wrong. It don't matter which way you look at it, you can't deny that." His shoulders and back tensed. They stared at each other, neither wanting to be the one to blink first. He waited for a moment or two then he continued talking.

"And, well, to show you I ain't kidding... to show you that I am serious about my child and his future... I'm even prepared to get married."

"Married?" The word leapt from my mouth. I felt as if I'd been hit in the stomach with an iron bar. I suddenly felt freezing cold, as if realising for the first time that the air conditioning was on too high. I shivered. Eleanor looked at him with her mouth wide open. She hadn't seen that coming. It was so strange for once to see her totally lost for words. It didn't last long, though.

"All that stuff you take's finally affected your brain. You're hallucinating," she said, recovering quickly.

Tyrone sucked his teeth again and came to stand next to me.

"Is it that I ain't good enough for you, Eleanor? Is that it?" he asked her looking right into her face. I looked at the floor, not wanting to be a part of any of this; wishing myself miles away. But Eleanor didn't flinch. She stared right back at him, even took a step nearer and leaned in towards him.

"Yes. Yes, that is it."

"Well, all right!" he said, laughing sarcastically. "Now we're getting to it. I've been good enough for a fling. Good enough to parade around in front of all your mates like I'm some kind of fucking trophy or souvenir you brought back from your holiday, but not good enough to marry!"

Eleanor turned away from him, from us. Her heels clacked as she crossed the room and took her turn again to stare out of the window. She spoke with her back to us, her voice seeming to come from a distance.

"You're young enough to be my son. Apart from some half-decent sex we've got nothing in common." She turned to face him. "Why on earth would I want to marry you?"

"Because we're having a child together! This situation, it's not just about us, is it? It's about bringing a kid into the world and giving him a steady home and a loving family. It's about giving him two parents that'll be there for him." He paused for a moment and I could see the hope in his eyes. And I knew that he really meant what he was saying; he really did. He did want to marry my mother. He gave a shy, half-grin.

"And we get on fine together. Don't we?"

Even I thought that was pushing it a bit given the atmosphere of the last week or so and Eleanor jumped at him.

"Oh, come on! You're talking rubbish, Tyrone. You knew the score. All this was a laugh, a bit of fun for both of us. It was all about us enjoying ourselves and having a good time not a warm-up for happy families."

"So all that you said to me... all the stuff about being special... about exciting you... bringing me here to be with you... now you're telling me you was lying to me?"

"That was just pillow talk!"

"So I don't mean nothing to you? Suddenly you don't like me no more?"

I saw her shoulders tense and a pulse in her cheek started to throb.

"Look, I've got a list of things to do before... before I'm fifty. And you were number three. In there between doing the anniversary vigil in Graceland and a bungee jump. *Number Three: young black dick.*"

I pulled my legs up on the chair and curled myself into a ball putting my hands over my ears.

"I don't want to hear this!" I shouted. "Too much information!" But Eleanor carried on; like a tsunami heading towards the shore, she was unstoppable.

"That's all it was. And you know that. I wanted a bit of rough and you were it."

"Eleanor, stop it!" I yelled at her as tears sprouted in my eyes. "Don't be so nasty to him. How can you say something like that?"

"It's okay, Vic," Tyrone said, putting his hand on my shoulder again in a gesture of comfort this time, before he turned back to Eleanor. "You ain't exactly no peach yourself, darling. Perhaps I've got a list of my own. Doing an old woman a favour, you know what I'm saying? I was with you because it was easy. Is that what you want to hear? Is it? You were easy, Eleanor. You. Were. Easy."

"Stop it, Tyrone!" I said, raising my head, my face and t-shirt now soaking wet with my tears. "Trading insults is getting us nowhere!"

"Well, who does she think she is? Talking to me like I was some piece of shit."

"She doesn't mean it. She's not herself, she's upset."

"Don't talk about me as if I wasn't here!" Eleanor said through gritted teeth. "Of course I'm upset. The last two weeks have been upsetting enough without today's last minute stand by Mr Responsible Parenthood. This pregnancy was never ever meant to happen. It's all been a huge mistake."

I leaned back in the chair and wiped my hand over my face. My head was throbbing and I closed my eyes as the memories of four months earlier came flooding back to me. Is that all it was? Today it felt like a lifetime.

Chapter Two

I'd decided to go into St John's that day to do some shopping with Megan. She was leaving for Canada the following weekend and wanted some souvenirs to take home for her mother and sister and some rum cake for her co-workers at the Toronto' CHUM Radio Station.

"Come with me and I'll stand you lunch at Hemingway's," she'd said, knowing that there was no way I was going to turn that down. So we'd jumped into the jeep she'd hired and zoomed into town together. Megan drove as if her arse was on fire; she hated changing down and so rather than brake and slow down and move down through the gears and then up again, she dodged around pot holes and charged through narrow gaps while I closed my eyes and held my breath and clutched the door handle for dear life, making all sorts of promises to God of good deeds I'd do if I got to St John's and back safely. She roared out laughing at my reactions.

"Why are your eyes closed? Don't you trust me?"

"I just wish you'd slow down a bit!"

"Driving fast's fun!" she insisted as she put her foot down to frustrate a boy-racer who was trying to overtake us in his noisy Nissan with its over-sized spoiler and go-faster stripe. He sounded the horn long and loud as he had to pull back behind us to avoid a lorry that was coming in the other direction. In spite of all that happened on the way in, we did, in fact, arrive in St John's in one piece and Megan backed the jeep into a parking space we'd been lucky enough to find in St Mary's Street. My legs felt weak as I got out, buckling under me and I had to grab the side of the vehicle for support.

"Just give me a minute," I said as I leaned against the jeep, not altogether jokingly. But with a burst of laughter Megan grabbed hold of my hand and pulled me down the street behind her. We took our time strolling through the stalls of the Vendors' Mall, where Megan bought the compulsory fridge magnets and a couple of t-shirts and then through Heritage Quay, where she spotted a beautiful mauve and blue dress for a wedding she was going to in Vancouver later in the year in the window of a smart boutique. We went inside and she tried it on. It looked stunning on her tall, slim yet shapely frame and so she bought it.

"At least nobody else will be wearing one the same!" she said.

I'd had a good look around in the same shop, which had some great stuff and I hadn't been able to resist a really cute ring and a gorgeous, flowing full-length beach dress that would double up in the evenings if I dressed it up a bit. There was a cruise ship in, but the streets weren't too busy and we enjoyed being able to shop in relative peace. We'd chatted with everyone that had served us; passing the time of day, discussing the rain that was forecast for that afternoon and how welcome it was after such a dry couple of weeks, and how sad we all were that the Christmas and New Year celebrations were over. Megan knew loads of people; her grandfather had been Antiguan and she'd visited the island on a regular basis since she was a child and her parents had bought their house in Jolly Harbour in the late 1990s as a holiday home, using the small inheritance her grandfather had left them as a deposit. Alan, her father, had since bought a piece of land near the south of the island where they hoped to build a retirement home one day soon. She was fun to be with and we'd hung out together most of the time since we'd met in the beauty salon just before Christmas. It wasn't that I didn't enjoy Eleanor's company because I did. We'd always been close as it had been just the two of us and we'd got on much better than many mothers and daughters. But she was always happy to just lie on the beach all day followed by having dinner in a restaurant at night and then go back to the house for drinks on the terrace with people we'd met at dinner or that she'd already made friends with. Most of them were couple and without exception, they were all in their forties and fifties. I'm not a party animal, in fact, I'm quite shy. In London I have a small circle of friends but most of my life revolves around Eleanor. I was just beginning to get bored with our holiday style and forever being with older people when Megan came along. She drove us to clubs and bars and rum shops and introduced me to a whole group of people I'd never have met if I'd stayed inside Jolly Harbour. And in spite of my shyness I had begun to come out of myself a bit and to really have some fun. I was going to miss her when she left. Eleanor and I were staying until the end of February when we had to return to London so that we could start the preparation for her next art exhibition, which was going to be held in a West End gallery in early September. While I loved Antigua, the prospect of spending the next two months there without Megan suddenly seemed a bit daunting.

Our lunch – we'd both had the shrimp pasta – was delicious and we'd washed it down with two lime daiquiris each. I know that was just a bit stupid but I honestly felt that alcohol couldn't make Megan's driving any worse than it already was. Emptying her glass, Megan took a look at her watch.

"It's half past two, hon. And it looks like the sky's about to open. Shall we get the bill and go?"

That proved a good idea as we were just getting into the jeep when the sky had turned a deep, dark gray and the predicted rain started to fall in big bouncing drops. By the time we reached Jolly Harbour it was a sheet of water that we ran through, getting soaked in the ten short paces from the jeep to the door of our villa. We burst into the house screaming and laughing and dropping water everywhere and then both stopped in our tracks at the sight of the gorgeous young guy in his boxers who was pouring two large drinks from the trolley next to the patio doors.

"Who the fuck are you?" I said dropping my bags on the floor and confronting him. "And what do you think you're doing?"

"Darling? Is that you?" Eleanor's voice drifted down the stairs.

"Are you talking to me?" I shouted back up to her.

"Of course I am!"

"Only there's a naked man... well, boy, actually, who's helping himself to our drinks. He seems quite at home here, thogh, so I thought perhaps you were talking to him," I couldn't resist adding.

"Oh, that's Tyrone," she called out in reply.

"Oh, well, I'm glad we cleared that up!" I looked back at him as he stood outlined against the wall-to-wall window.

"Ladies, the pleasure's all mine," Tyrone said, smiling and sweeping past us, a drink in each hand. "No need for that, baby," he said to Megan, who'd grabbed a knife from the open-plan work top that separated the kitchen from the rest of the room as soon as she'd seen him, and then he climbed the stairs two at a time, leaving

30

us to watch the rippling muscles in his back and his tight buttocks, and breathe in the sweet smell of weed that drifted behind him.

Megan collapsed in a heap of laughter onto the sofa and kicked off her shoes. I went for towels to dry us and the pools of water we'd left covering the floor.

"You've got to give it to her," Megan said, rigorously drying her huge mass of tight black curls. "I mean most women her age are positively elderly and past it. She's so glamorous, especially compared to my mom. I'm sure she stopped having sex with my father years ago. And I'm sure he's been her only lover; she's never had it with anyone else, yet alone a babe like him."

"Would you like her for a while?" I asked, referring to Eleanor, only half-jokingly. "Sometimes she's an embarrassment."

"Oh, come on! You've got to admire the way she rolls. You wouldn't say no to a romp with him, would you? Cos I know I wouldn't. Christ! Did you see those shoulders? And the eyes? And the butt?"

"So you have to ask yourself, what he's doing with a woman old enough to be his mother," I said. "I mean, what was he, nineteen?"

"No way! He's older than that. Twenty-four or twenty-five I'd say."

"Yes, and she's forty-three."

"Well, if it was the other way round, say, your dad was dating a girl who was sixteen or seventeen years younger you wouldn't say anything at all."

"I would! I'm twenty-two. I wouldn't expect my dad to date someone close to my age. If I knew who he was, of course," I couldn't resist adding.

"Sorry, hon," Megan said, putting her arm around me. "I forgot about that."

I'd told her about my parents the second night we'd hung out together. They'd both been students at the same art college and when my mum found out she was pregnant, my dad, who she said was two years older than her, graduated two months later and left her to drop out and face the birth and bringing me up all alone. Whenever I'd asked Eleanor about him she refused to talk. Just said he was worthless and a good-for-nothing she should have known better than to get involved with and that we were better off without him.

"How about a drink?" I said, trying to lighten the mood. "It might distract us from what's going on upstairs."

"I'm always up for a drink. Shame we didn't go to my place. We could have hung out there and not disturbed Eleanor and her guy. But it's still raining too hard for us to go anywhere."

"No problem," I said, opening the patio door and stepping onto the veranda. "We're sheltered here under the awning and once I close the door," I slid it across behind us, "we can shut them out."

We spent the afternoon swinging in the hammocks, looking through the slowly diminishing rain, beyond the pool, across the sand and at the sea, listening to music and talking about everything and nothing while working our way down a bottle of coconut rum that we mixed with pineapple juice until we suddenly realised that it was dark. And that the rain had stopped. And that Eleanor was still upstairs with her young boy.

And she stayed upstairs with him for two days.

When they finally emerged I felt awkward and uncomfortable, like an outsider suddenly. I was like Ms Prim and Proper, the wallflower who was looking on in disapproval; a bitter old-maid disgusted and horrified by another woman's behaviour. It was as if we'd swapped places; Eleanor was the carefree young woman who was throwing caution to the wind as she entered into a passionate affair with abandon, while I tutted and looked sour, shook my head and told myself it would all end in tears.

Eleanor was an amazing woman who had always been a free spirit; bringing me up alone hadn't been easy for her as she struggled to earn a living teaching art while juggling childcare and making quality time for us to be together. And it was a good time, a fun time, a magical time. She was a brilliant mother, making me the envy of all my friends and we loved each other madly; there was nobody else in the world but the two of us as far as we were both concerned. She must have been disappointed when I didn't show the slightest inclination towards drawing or painting but she filled my life with love and huge hugs and the hosepipe in the garden and feeding ducks in the park and paddling at the seaside and ice-creams and stories and cuddling up on the sofa watching films and singing together in the bath and the car. There were no men that I remember; no stream of *uncles* coming into and out of our lives, which might explain why she was making up for lost time now with Tyrone.

Then, when I was thirteen, she sold her first paintings. She had always loved London with a passion and for several years, late at night once I was asleep, she'd been painting abstracts of the city's landscapes and famous landmarks. She bucked up the courage one day to put some on e-bay and to her delighted astonishment they sold quickly and for far more than she'd ever imagined. Interest in her work suddenly began to grow, especially after Barbara Buchanan, a TV celebrity, bought one of her paintings and Tweeted about it. Very soon, galleries that had never heard of her were clamouring to show her work. She gave interviews in magazines, newspapers and on the radio. A television company made a high profile documentary about her and her unique style, describing her as the UK's most promising, prolific artist of the Noughties. She became a guest on chat-shows and quizzes. She was soon a very recognisable, familiar face and she took to her newly-found celebrity like she'd been born to it. Within three years her paintings were selling for hundreds of thousands of pounds and she'd bought a glorious Georgian house in Whitechapel for us and when I left school with very disappointing A Level results and no desire to re-sit them or go to university, I started working for her as her PA.

And so our roles became reversed. It was now my turn to take care of her by organising her diary and running the office and house. I think we were both very pleasantly surprised at how efficient and good I was at my new job.

"You were always bossy," Eleanor said one day as I hung up the phone after telling a journalist that the earliest interview Eleanor could give him was in three weeks time and if he didn't decide there and then he'd lose that spot, too, as we had writers queuing up for a chance to talk to her.

But I loved what I did. Although technically Eleanor was my boss I was pretty much in charge and I thrived on the independence that gave me and the responsibility I had. But most of all I loved it because I was doing it for her. I was finally able to give something back to the woman who had sacrificed so much and worked so hard for me. I took away the every-day worries and stresses, making sure everything around her ran like clockwork, liberating her from the humdrum, day-to-day tasks so that she had the freedom to paint and to enjoy herself.

And enjoy herself she did.

But this fling, this affair, with Tyrone, was something I'd never seen before. Eleanor had turned into a forty-three-year-old wild child who was fast getting out of control. She and Tyrone spent every single moment together. They went off to the beaches on the Atlantic coast of Antigua, out to eat in a different restaurant every night, and made loud, wild love in her room – while I put my fingers in my ears or the pillow over my head, or by the pool – when I was inside faking a siesta – and on the deserted beach behind our villa at night, not caring who might see them. Megan had left and I felt completely alone. Without her I didn't really have the confidence to go to bars and clubs or even restaurants. I bought supplies from the supermarket and cooked for myself at home. I didn't even like going onto the beach on my own so I stayed at the villa, sitting by the pool, reading and fielding phone calls from Rhonda, Eleanor's agent, who was anxious to speak to her.

"Where the hell is she? You've been telling me she's not available for three days now!" Rhonda had growled down the phone at me.

"She's just having a complete rest; that's why we're here. You can talk to me if it's urgent," I said. Well, I could hardly say *'She's upstairs shagging a local beach bum, who's young enough to be her son.'* could I?

"It's really not that urgent," Rhonda conceded. So why was she continually ringing then? "It's only to touch base really, you know, and confirm our meeting with the gallery owners when she gets back."

"Yes, she knows. It's in the diary. Of course she'll call you, if not from here then as soon as we're back in London."

"Everything is alright, isn't it? You seem a little... distant. Sort of subdued," Rhonda added.

"I'm fine. I'm relaxed and chilled, that's what it is. We're just having a lovely holiday. The villa's super luxurious and it's right on the beach. The weather's glorious. What more could we ask for?"

"Well, as long as you're sure," she added before hanging up.

And so that was the pattern of our days, through January and into February. Every so often I'd take a taxi into St John's and walk around drinking in the sights and the sounds and the smells of the city. Once or twice I ventured down into Jolly Harbour alone in the evening to eat, always accompanied by my Kindle so that I didn't feel quite so lonely, and because I didn't want anyone to feel sorry for me and feel they had to start talking to me. In my own way I was enjoying my martyrdom.

Every once in a while Eleanor would make an effort to have breakfast with me or ask me what I was going to do that day. Once or twice she even suggested that I join her and Tyrone on whatever they were planning to do. I always refused. It was bad enough being gooseberry in the villa without being a spare part watching their teenage antics on the beach or in a restaurant or bar as well.

Then suddenly, they stopped going out for the day and Eleanor took to going onto the beach behind the villa in the afternoon, just for an hour or so, alone, to paint. Tyrone stayed by the pool, sleeping in the hammock under the canopy while she sat on a rock, brush in hand, losing herself in her talent. Most mornings, though, she was nursing a hangover. She carried the smell of weed about her now, and she'd lost a bit of weight. She obviously didn't need to eat – she was feeding on love.

Chapter Three

With just a week to go before we were due to leave, Eleanor came down to breakfast dressed in a long, elegant cream sundress with large red flowers around the flowing skirt, the colours showing off her golden tan beautifully. Her light brown hair, which was now a gorgeous honey-blonde thanks to the sun, was held back with a large comb and for once she smelt of Guerlain's Shalimar, her favourite perfume and not marijuana. In spite of the huge sunglasses that completely hid her eyes, I took this as a good sign; she almost looked like her old self!

"I'm going into town, I've got a couple of errands to do," she announced.

"Oh, I'll come!"

"No!"

I looked at her: that had been a bit of a sharp retort.

"You'd be bored, darling," she said, realising she'd hurt my feelings. "I'm just going to the travel agent's to see if I can book Tyrone on our flight back to London. I've invited him to come and stay for a few days or so."

"Oh, brilliant!" I said.

"What's the matter? You're not going to be difficult about this, are you? Surely I can invite a friend to stay if I want to, can't I? The house is big enough for you not to even know he's there."

"It's not that. It's just... well... you've got your exhibition to prepare for. You'll be busy. Rhonda's on the phone twice a day reminding me of meetings and things we have to do as soon as we're back." Okay! I know I was exaggerating!

"It's not until September, is it? I've got plenty of time. And besides, he's only coming for a couple of weeks."

"You just said I few days..." She shrugged and tutted at my interruption.

"A few days or a few weeks, it doesn't matter, does it? I can get on with my painting once he's gone. Although the main work for the exhibition was completed months ago, as you well know, or I wouldn't have even entertained the idea of taking two months off to come here, would I?"

I topped up my coffee cup, bit into my croissant and didn't reply. She leaned across the table and squeezed my hand.

"Look, I know you've probably felt a little bit out of it lately. You know... with Tyrone..." she nodded her head towards the top floor of the villa where he was, presumably, still sleeping. "But I'm enjoying myself so much." She gave a wry smile and for a moment looked young and girly. "And I simply want to spend more time with him so it makes sense for him to come to London for a while, doesn't it? But he's not taking your place, is he? Nobody could ever take your place, could they? Eh?"

I shrugged my shoulders, not prepared to give an inch. I could be as stubborn as she was when I wanted to. And I knew that she wanted to take him to London so that she could show him off like a hunter returning from a safari with a tiger's skin.

"Let's go out to dinner tonight the three of us!" she said, as if she was telling me I'd just won a prize. "You and Tyrone haven't really got to know each other, have you?"

"Well, I've hardly had the opportunity to, have I? You rarely venture out of the bedroom. He's like a ghost I occasionally pass on the stairs."

"Don't be childish, Victoria! Several times we've gone out to join you at the pool and you've always collected up your things and come straight in."

"That's because I had something to do!" I replied hotly.

"Or you didn't like the idea of me enjoying myself?"

"No! It wasn't that! I just don't like to see my mother practically fucking some beach bum young enough to be her son next to me in the water!"

She took her sunglasses off and stared at me. Her eyes, in spite of the Eye Dew I know she'd have used, looked red and heavy.

"Please don't use that language. There's absolutely no need for you to be coarse and crude. All we were doing was messing around and splashing each other. It's called *having fun*. You should try it some time," she added, scathingly.

I ignored her and took another sip of my coffee. Yes, she might be having fun, but I wasn't. Now I was counting the days until we left.

She sighed deeply and put her shades back on. "I'll book a table somewhere nice, tonight. Where would you like to go? Sugar Ridge?"

"I'd quite like to go somewhere small and local," I said. "Perhaps Taco Loco, or the new seafood restaurant. Or somewhere that's beachside. One of the restaurants at Dickinson Bay would be nice."

Her expression of surprise that I wanted to venture outside Jolly Harbour didn't need words.

"Well, yes. Okay. If that's what you want." She looked at her watch and jumped up. "I have to go. See you later." And with that she was gone. I wondered why she was in such a hurry to get to the travel agents', especially when I could have booked Tyrone's flight on the Virgin website for her. I gave a mental shrug as I heard her start up the hire car and was just about to take my coffee cup and plate to the dishwasher when Tyrone appeared at the bottom of the stairs in a pair of designer boxers. His *dawn horn* evident beneath them caused me to blush and look away but he'd already seen my reaction. He gave a wry smile and I blushed even more, absolutely furious with myself.

"Good day," he said, rubbing his hands over his bare chest. He strolled down the side corridor and into the ground-floor bathroom where he had a wee, noisily and with the door wide open; he was obviously aware that I could hear him. I was determined to ignore him and his loutish behaviour and took a pretend swig from my empty cup as he sauntered back to the table. He checked out the coffee pot and seeing that there was still some inside, he poured himself a cup. Then, suddenly aware of the filthy look I was giving him he withdrew his outstretched hand from the pile of croissants.

"Okay if I help myself?" he asked. I shrugged. I couldn't care less whether he had one or not, I just resented his continual taking and that now included something as trivial as a croissant.

"I take it that was a yes, then?" he said, leaning forward and taking one from the pile, breaking it open and sending crumbs all over the table. I tutted loudly.

"Oh, sorry!" He stood up and strolled into the kitchen to get a cloth and a plate. Every cell in his body screamed *'cocky and arrogant'*. I hated him with a vengeance, yet I had to admit he was rather gorgeous. If you liked that sort of thing. And I didn't. I waited until he came back to the table, until the moment he sat down after brushing the crumbs and catching them on the plate, and then, in a deliberate snub stood up and walked back into the kitchen.

"I take it you don't want no deep and meaningful conversation with me this morning then?" he called after me, chuckling to himself at his own wit.

"I just don't think we have anything to say to each other, do we? You've probably got even less in common with me than you have with Eleanor. What could we possibly find to talk about? Nothing at all!" Why was I even giving him the time of day?

"We probably got a lot in common. We both young, we both grew up in London. Your mum."

I flew back into the living room too angry to realise I'd fallen right into his trap.

"My mum? My mum? Don't you dare talk to me about her! We haven't got her *in common* as you so nicely put it! I'm her daughter but you! You're... you're just some drop out with no morals who's letting her pay-role him! You think you know her? Well, you don't! And what are you suggesting? Eh? That I sit and listen while you give me all the details of everything the two of you have been getting up to for the last two months? Do you think that's clever? Are you proud of yourself?" I stopped, breathing heavily. I was livid. And he grinned at me, which wound me up even more.

"You're a good-looking girl, the image of your mum. But you're uptight all the time and you look miserable. You need to chill, Babe," he said, sitting back in the chair and looking at me through half-closed eyes, his voice taking on a London accent now. He switched from educated-London to street-Estuary to Antiguan as the impulse took him, his personality morphing to accompany the accent. He seemed to think that I'd see what we actually did have in common if he talked more like me.

"I am not your Babe. And don't even try to tell me what I need to do!"

"I'm just saying. Why are you so worked up about me and your mum?" He kept on saying *'your mum'* in a deliberate attempt to wind me up even further. He knew I always called her Eleanor.

"I don't like to see her making a fool of herself for a start!"

"Mekin a fool a sheself?" He flipped back into dialect. "How she doing that?" He stared at me, daring me to answer him. I rose to the challenge.

"You're... what?... twenty?"

"Twenty-five."

"And she's forty-three! Or has she told you she's younger than that?" I spat at him. "What are you doing with a woman of forty-three?"

"Having fun." He paused to sip his coffee. "At forty-three she's a woman in her prime." He peered into the cup before taking another long sip. "Or is it the fact that we're having fun, that she's enjoying herself that's upsetting you?"

"Oh, shut up!" I said and stormed back into the kitchen only for him to follow me. I leaned against the sink for a moment and then I turned round to find him standing right there, only two feet from me. He held my gaze.

"I can understand that you might be wondering what I'm doing with a more mature lady..."

"Oh, I'm not wondering, I know! I can hear you through the wall most of the time!"

He laughed and shook his head. I felt about fourteen.

"I'm not talking about sex," he said with a stupid grin on his face. "Although, that's obviously a part of it, I won't deny that."

"You're getting all you can from her in every way. For the last two months she's kept you; she's fed you, taken you out, bought you clothes and now she's giving you a free holiday in London. That's what you're doing with a more mature lady. It's not exactly hard to work out!"

"Let me ask you something, Vic."

I waited for his trick question.

"Do you think I'm forcing your mum to be with me? Does it look like she's not enjoying herself with me?"

I moved past him back towards the living room; I pushed open the door and stepped back out onto the patio and threw myself down onto one of the hammocks. I needed air. But he wasn't going to let me off the hook so easily and so he followed me and sat down right next to me, the force of his body setting us off in a violent swing.

"Come on! You haven't answered me. Is your mum having a good time with me or not?"

"I couldn't possibly say!"

"Oh, you couldn't possibly say, shit! You can see she's having a great time. She's told me she's having the best time in years. So what's wrong with that? Huh? Why shouldn't your mum have some fun? Or are you too selfish to want that for her?"

"Don't you call me selfish! You know nothing about Eleanor and me or our relationship. Nothing!"

"She's a classy lady and we like each other. I might not know nothing about the two of you, but it seems to me that you might be just a little bit jealous that she's getting some sexual action when you're not."

Without realising what I was doing I'd lifted my arm back to slap his face but he'd seen it coming and grabbed my forearm tightly, stopping the blow, and held onto it.

"Whoa! No need for that! What? You think slapping me's gonna change anything? Am I gonna tell her to go cancel my ticket to London because I almost got a slap?" He had a huge grin on his face.

"Don't you laugh at me!" I said, wrestling my arm free.

"Then stop behaving like a spoilt child! You're a big woman now."

Hating myself for doing it, I burst into tears. Huge sobs took over my body and I couldn't stop myself. Before I realised it he'd put his arm around my shoulder and had pulled me towards him. I cried onto his bare shoulder for what seemed like an eternity. I'd never have guessed I had so many tears inside me and I couldn't even have told you why I was crying. Finally, the sobs slowed down and faded away. I pulled away from him, horrified at my behaviour and that I'd let him comfort me. I felt so foolish. He stood up and crossed to one of the patio chairs and brought me a towel that had been hanging on the back of it.

"Here, dry your face," he said handing it to me and sitting on the floor this time, next to my feet, so that we were facing each other. I rubbed the towel over my eyes and face and then down my neck and chest, which were soaked. "There's nothing to cry for."

"What do you know?" I said. "I've already told you that you know nothing about us."

"I know that Eleanor loves and adores you. I know that she couldn't manage without you, that you've always been more than a daughter, more than a PA, more than she could ever have hoped and wished for. You're her everything; her reason for being. Believe me, you are."

I looked at him stunned, waiting for the put-down, for a sign of the cocky bastard, but there was none.

"How do you know that?"

"Because she's told me."

"She's discussed me with you?" I was appalled to think Eleanor would have talked about me with this creep; this... this... gigolo.

"She loves you. She's your mum and she's really proud of you. You're her main topic of conversation."

"Yeah, right!"

"You are! Straight up!"

"Well, that's nice to know!"

"Vic, don't be like that! It's true that she is feeling a bit guilty because she's spent so much time with me over the last coupla weeks. She wants you to enjoy yourself. She thought you'd be out doing things once you'd hooked up with Megan. She didn't know you'd prefer to be on your own."

"She knew Megan was only here for Christmas!"

"Yeah, but Megan introduced you to other people..."

"That didn't mean I was going clubbing or hanging out with them once she left. Eleanor knows I'm a home bird. I don't even go out in London with people I've known all my life."

"So, what's the problem, then? If you don't go out in London and you don't want to go out here, what you crying for?"

"Nothing!"

"Is it cos your mum's having sex and you're not?"

"Jesus! Don't be so gross!"

"I got a coupla friends I could hook you up with."

"No! I'm not some charity case! I'll fix up my own dates, thank you! I don't want you to arrange sex with some stranger for me like I'm some kind of loser. Just who do you think you are? I don't want sex at all!"

"Well, that's what it looks like to me. You're mum's getting sexed up every night and you're not. Sounds like just plain jealousy you're suffering from."

"Well, you're wrong!" I screeched at him, jumping to my feet. He strained his neck and squinted his eyes as he looked up at me from his sitting position.

"So, what's up with you, then? Why you causing all this fuss?"

"Because I don't like to see her taken for a ride by the likes of you!"

"The likes of me? And what's that then *the likes of me*?"

"A beach bum! A bloke who spends his life pimping off rich older women. You're no more than a rent boy."

"I ain't no gay for pay!"

"Well, gigolo, then!"

In one swift movement he was on his feet and moving towards me. I had nowhere to go as I was now on the edge of the pool.

"Let's get one thing straight, Miss High and Mighty. I don't sell myself to no-one. Got that?" He prodded me in the chest and I could see that he was angry. I braced myself, afraid that he'd nudge me into the water. "Eleanor, your mother, started all of this. She started it all the day we met. I was sitting on the beach talking to my friends, sharing a little smoke, when she come up and asked me to put some lotion on her back. You understand me? SHE came up to ME. I earn my living pushing weed. That's a fact of life and I can't change it. But if people didn't ask for it, I wouldn't be able to sell it, would I? But I don't pimp off no women. Eleanor's offered me all these things and I ain't gonna say no. But that don't make me any less than you. You got that?"

I nodded. I wasn't afraid of him, but I didn't want to push him, after all, in spite of living in close proximity with him for two months, I didn't know him or anything about him and his sudden mood change had unnerved me. I turned and went back inside, up to my room to shower and lie down. I had a headache and I felt lousy, aware that I'd probably made a complete fool of myself and that right now he was probably laughing to himself about me. The room was cool and dark, but after lying down for ten minutes or so the headache showed no sign of lifting so I went down into the kitchen where I knew there were some Paracetamol in one of the cupboards. Tyrone was lying outside in the hammock. He heard me in the kitchen and came inside.

"Look, I'm sorry about all that earlier, Vic. I sorta feel we've got off on the wrong foot you and me."

I filled my glass with water, popped two tablets into my mouth and took a big swig to swallow them.

"Can't we start again?" he asked. "Like two civilised people?"

I rinsed the glass and turned to face him.

"Please?" he said. "Let me make us a little drink as a goodwill gesture." He held out his little finger to me. "Make up? Like in school? You remember that?"

I was too exhausted to argue any more. And in spite of myself I laughed. I laughed and hooked my little finger into his and we shook.

"Look, I know what it probably looks like to you, but I ain't out to leech off Eleanor, okay? She's one hot lady and we're having fun.

And if she wants to give me little presents and a holiday in England, well... I ain't gonna say no, am I? But that's all there is. I like her. She's a real lady and I ain't met too many of them, you know what I mean? And I know, just like she knows that in a coupla weeks she'll send me packing back here. It's a holiday romance. That's all. You understand? You have nothing at all to worry about."

I nodded and gave a little sigh.

"Good! Now, let me get you that drink."

"I don't want a little drink. Well, nothing alcoholic; I've got a headache," I said. "But some of your mum's ginger beer sounds good."

His smile could have lit up the whole island.

"You like Mommy's ginger beer?"

"It's the best I've ever tasted," I said. I'd churlishly refused some when he'd first brought it to us in two large Coca Cola bottles, but as Eleanor had waxed lyrical about it I'd secretly tried some one day when they were out and to my surprise I'd been amazed by just how great it was.

"Mommy's ginger beer's famous all over the island. And her sorrel wine. She's gonna be happy when I tell her you like it," he said, pouring two big glasses and carrying them out onto the patio ahead of me. He made himself comfortable in the hammock again and I sat back in one of the comfy chairs. We sipped our ginger beer in a friendly silence that said more than any deep conversation ever could.

Chapter Four

Eleanor came back an hour or so later and found us both splashing around in the pool. She stepped out through the patio doors, stopped and stared at us in a very exaggerated way, her mouth wide open.

"Well! Perhaps I should have gone off for the morning and left the two of you alone weeks ago. What's brought on the *entente-cordiale*?" she asked, crossing to the side of the pool and leaning down, knowing that Tyrone would swim over, expertly raise himself from the pool in one swift, athletic movement and plant a kiss on her lips. Which he did.

"We just decided it's better to be friends. We don't wanna be vexed with each other all the time," Tyrone said, by way of explanation.

She kicked off her shoes and lowered herself to sit at the edge of the pool, dangling her feet in the water.

"Well, that's good news," she said, smiling at both of us. But there was something about the smile that didn't quite go all the way to her eyes; I know her too well and I knew that for some reason she wasn't totally happy about something. Didn't she want us to get on? Was there any pleasing her?

"Did you get me on the flight?" Tyrone asked, holding onto her ankles and pushing himself back and forth through the water, the sun gleaming off his back.

Eleanor looked at him vacantly for a second and then she seemed to snap to and realise what he was talking about.

51

"Oh, there were so many people in the travel agent's that I decided to look online later. Or perhaps you could, darling?" she asked turning to me.

"No problem," I said, smiling. "I'll do it in a bit."

"See if you can get him in Upper Class with us, would you?"

"Fucking hell! I'm travelling in Upper Class?" Tyrone's pleasure at this new experience was touching. He stretched his arm forward, grabbed Eleanor's hand and in an unexpectedly tender gesture, placed a kiss in the palm. She smiled down at him.

"It's so damn hot!" she complained. And with one swift movement peeled her dress up over her head and slid into the water wearing just her knickers; breasts sitting up pertly, nipples hard and erect. She ducked under the water and came up with her arms around Tyrone, rubbing her body against his.

I had to smile to myself, although their behaviour made me uncomfortable. I could see she was being territorial; she was showing me that he belonged to her. She couldn't be jealous of the thought of the two of us getting on, surely?

Feeling like the old-maid chaperone again I decided to leave them both to it. I swam to the steps and got out of the pool, put my sarong around my swimsuit and went inside to fix a big salad for lunch for all of us. They didn't even notice I'd gone.

From then on, I'd got on reasonably well with Tyrone. He had been right; we did have quite a bit in common, or at least we seemed to, always chatting animatedly about politics and world affairs which were two subjects that really interested him and he felt passionately about. He cared passionately about people and about equality and I couldn't help feeling that with a push in the right direction he could have a future as a politician. But when they were together I still kept out of their way most of the time. Liking Tyrone, or rather disliking him less, didn't change the fact that I didn't want to watch the two of them continually touching and kissing each other. I was mindful, too, that the holiday was almost over and wanted to get back into work mode so that returning to London wouldn't be such a shock. But I did go out to dinner with the pair of them a couple of times before we left and saw more evidence that Tyrone was good company, amusing and entertaining, and it was obvious that he did genuinely care for Eleanor. She, in turn, behaved outrageously with him, forever draping herself around him and stroking his face and arms and shoulders, especially if she saw anyone giving them a disapproving look; then there was no stopping her. She'd taken him into town one morning and bought him a complete new wardrobe for his holiday to London. I hadn't thought that was really necessary as Tyrone usually dressed okay in a sort of casual, beachy way, but I kept my mouth well and truly shut. He had looked vaguely embarrassed when they'd got back from the shopping spree laden with bags and Eleanor was showing me all they'd bought.

"As soon as we get to London we'll get you something heavier," she said. "You'll need a couple of decent jackets and sweaters."

Eleanor had driven Tyrone to his mother's house to pick up his suitcase. While being hospitable, the woman, apparently, made no secret of the fact that she didn't exactly approve of her son dating a white woman who was only a year younger than she was.

"Well, she might only be a year older than me, but she looks at least ten or fifteen," Eleanor said when we were chatting in the hammocks later that afternoon.

"That's a bit unkind," I said, shaking my head in disbelief at what she'd said. "She's had a much harder life than you have."

"I was a single mother, too, don't forget!"

"Yes, but she brought up four kids, didn't she? You only brought up one."

"She didn't bring up Tyrone. He spent most of his childhood in England with his father."

"But you had all sorts of things to help and make life easier for you. She didn't. And you got some help, like family allowance and such which I bet weren't available here."

Eleanor shrugged; Tyrone's mother and her struggles weren't her concern.

"The point I'm making is that she seemed sort of... well... *matronly*. She was wearing what I can only describe as a *frock*, and she's fat."

The biggest crime you could commit as far as Eleanor was concerned was to be overweight. Even slightly. Serial killers and suicide bombers were looked upon more kindly than the obese.

"She's really let herself go," Eleanor continued, determined to finish her hatchet job on the poor woman. "Very old fashioned. But then it's hard to be fashionable when you're that size, I suppose."

"Oh, come on! Look at some of the women we've seen here! They're big but they're really great dressers."

"Well, some are. If you like that sort of thing, you know, tight clothes and all that," she said. "But she didn't seem at all grateful that I was taking her son on a free holiday," she added, referring to Tyrone's mother again.

I wonder why?

"How long will Tyrone be staying with us? I mean, I know his ticket's open, but do you have any idea? Have you got any plans?"

"He'll probably stay until the middle of summer. He likes tennis, apparently he played a bit at school and he's mad about the Williams Sisters so it would be so nice to be able to take him to Wimbledon or Queen's."

My face probably showed my surprise, as that meant he'd be staying for at least three months. This morning she'd said a couple of days, then a couple of weeks. Now it was three months. Eleanor noticed and jumped back in.

"But, we'll take it as it comes, there's no need to look like that."

"I'm not looking like anything. I just don't want him to get in the way of your exhibition."

"He won't. That's not until September. And stop being my mother! Do you think I'd let anything or anyone get in the way of my exhibition? I can't believe you said that, you know how hard I work and what it means to me! But, exhibition aside, I like him being around, understood?" she snapped.

"Completely!" I snapped back.

The following day was our last and in the late afternoon I took a jug of Mommy's ginger beer from the fridge and poured myself a large glass, which I took out to the patio to watch my last Antiguan sunset.

As I stepped through the patio doors the sight of it took my breath away. All around and above me the huge sky was turning mauve around the edges, with orange and pink reflections from the golden sphere that was touching the edge of the horizon, streaking the clouds. I turned to my right and took in the splendid sight of the rippling green hills which formed the range known as Sleeping Indian, because that's what they looked like from a distance, before turning back and walking past the pool and down through the small gate onto the deserted beach. It felt as if the sea had hypnotised me and now I was under its spell it was beckoning me, calling me to it. I crossed the sand and stood with the water lapping my ankles watching the sun slowly slip into the sea miles ahead of me in the distance. A huge sigh of pleasure rippled through my body.

"I love this place," I heard myself say out loud and I realised with a surge of surprise that it was true. It was beautiful beyond comparison. The beaches were the stuff of travel posters; the weather, a temperamental diva - big, outlandish, warm and awesome, just like the people; the vegetation lush and every conceivable shade and tone of green with flowers, fruits and plants adding magnificent splashes of colour; the rainbows after the tropical showers were bigger and brighter than any I'd ever seen elsewhere. It was a magical place. And tomorrow we were leaving. I felt my throat catch and my eyes moisten, which amazed me as I'd spent most of the last few weeks wishing I was back in London. I brushed a tear away as I smelled a familiar sweetness and then heard the sand rustle behind me.

"You gonna miss this, Vic?" Tyrone asked as he came to stand beside me, holding a can of beer in one hand and a joint in the other. I nodded my reply, afraid I might cry if I spoke my response.

"Me, too."

We stood in silence, both lost in the deep beauty of the sunset ahead of us, watching until the sun had completely disappeared.

"No green flash tonight," he said breaking the stillness.

"Green flash? What's that?"

"It's some kind of phenomenon that happens when the sun sets. The moment, the very second it disappears there's like a green flash."

"Really?" I said, turning my head back towards the horizon in the vain hope I might see it.

"Yup! I don't understand the science of it but it's supposed to be something that only happens here in the Caribbean."

"It must be amazing. Is it?"

"I don't know. I ain't never seen it," he laughed.

I looked at him, unsure whether to believe him or not. He smiled and took a long, final draw on his joint before burying the tiny remains in the sand.

"Look, Vic, in spite of everything, you not liking me... not trusting me... and I can understand that," he added quickly to stop me butting in, " But, you know... I hope we're friends."

"Of course we are," I said smiling, surprised to realise that I meant it. He looked into my face to check I was telling the truth.

"Good!" he said, after a couple of moments, when he saw that I really was being honest.

And we walked back towards the villa to get ready for our last supper. We were spending it together in Jolly Harbour, Eleanor, Tyrone and me.

Chapter Five

And so we came back to London, the three of us together. First of all, I didn't see that much of Tyrone; I had my own wing of the house, which consisted of my bedroom, my bathroom, my office and a small living-room with a fridge, freezer, microwave, TV and sink. He was sharing Eleanor's bedroom even though there were three empty ones. I didn't see why he couldn't have used one of those to hang his clothes. It would have given both of them some privacy and he could have still spent every night in her bed, but I'd given a mental shrug ages ago where they were concerned; it really wasn't any of my business and neither of them seemed to want any privacy from the other. And besides, I was busy getting on with my job and my life. Starved of cultural events for nearly three months, I went to the theatre and or a concert almost every night and left the love birds to it.

Now he was away from Antigua, Tyrone decided to up his beach-boy alter ego; to show the whole of London his Caribbean roots. He wore a bright turquoise or Rasta coloured du-rag over his locks and walked with a low, exaggerated, stroll, calling everyone *'mah brudda'* or *'mon'* and overdoing the Caribbean accent. Eleanor took him everywhere with her; to meetings, interviews, shopping, her studio, introducing him as her *'significant other'*. Photos of the two of them out and about had appeared in the Metro and Evening Standard and even one or two of the nationals and gossip mags. It had apparently been his birthday the previous week and she'd taken him shopping and bought him a bracelet and a Rolex watch. I thought I'd remembered him telling me once that his birthday was in September.

"One for each wrist!" she'd joked as the three of us toasted his birthday in champagne before the two of them went out to dinner. I caught Tyrone's eye over the rim of his champagne flute and he immediately lowered his gaze. He knew what I was thinking - he'd sell or pawn them both as soon as he got back home. Still, I gave a mental shrug; I suppose they were his and he could do as he liked with them.

Yet in spite of insisting he made her happier than any man she'd ever met, Eleanor was suddenly becoming increasingly snappy with him. She now seemed to be critical of the very things that had attracted her to him; things that I'd seen from the beginning.

"Why don't you go out for a while? See something of London? Go visit your father?" she asked him one morning in the middle of a meeting she and I were having about a request for a commission from an ageing rock star who was marrying a Lithuanian model several years younger than his sons.

"I'm just fine here," he said, stretching out the full length of the sofa. "You said we going out for dinner tonight."

"That's tonight. It's only ten fifteen in the morning now. You've more than enough time to get to Rainham and back."

He'd sucked his teeth and carried on watching the screen. Conversation over. Another time she broached the subject of what work he would do when he returned home. He looked at her through half-opened lids, unsure of whether she was joking or not.

"Something will turn up. When the time comes," he said. She'd tutted and sighed before striding out of the room, slamming the door behind her. Then when he did go out she didn't like it. He'd taken her advice and gone back to some old haunts. Although he'd only been fourteen at the time, he'd been very street-wise and his father had sent him back to Antigua because he was mixing with what his father considered to be *the Wrong Crowd.* So, he'd looked up a couple of his mates from school and hadn't come home until lunch-time the following day. Eleanor had been incandescent with rage. She'd rung him so many times he'd switched his phone off. Then when he'd finally strolled in, eyes red, smelling of booze and weed, she'd screamed at him for half an hour that he was ungrateful, an oaf and a waste of space and then thrown herself into his arms and disappeared back to her room with him for the rest of the afternoon.

When he wasn't prostrate on the sofa in front of the TV, he'd be in the basement where we had our own modest gym, working on keeping himself in good physical shape. At times he'd go out for a jog. Once or twice he invited me along as he knew I jogged, too, but I always refused as I knew I'd only hold him back and besides, Eleanor hadn't looked too pleased when he'd suggested I went with him. Sometimes Eleanor would join him in the gym, but although she loved being with him and taking him out and about, she was starting to spend more time in her studio, alone.

I'd come home from a trip to the bank one morning in mid-April.

"Hey, Vic, what's up?" Tyrone called out loudly as he heard me come in the front door. "Come sit by me!"

I crossed the hall, my heels clacking on the oak floorboards and instead of going up the main staircase to my room, I turned into a doorway on the right and there he was; mobile phone in one hand and TV remote in the other. Eleanor had bought him a sim card for his phone and kept it topped up for him so he spent a lot of time calling home and, of course, speaking in dialect. This also wound her up because she didn't know what he was saying but why would a conversation between him and Mommy or one of his friends be of interest to her?

"How's it hanging?"

"I'm okay, just busy," I said, slipping off my jacket as the warmth of the room hit me. Tyrone always had the heat set on at least twenty-five degrees. "Where's Eleanor."

"In she studio."

"She's painting?" I asked, surprised because her work for the exhibition was complete.

"Me dun nah wha she fa do."

His tone surprised me.

"Have you two fallen out?" I asked, curious, in spite of my promise to myself to stay out of their lives and not get involved in or comment on their relationship. He shrugged.

"Only, there seems to have been a bit of... well, at bit of an atmosphere, lately," I said, when he remained silent.

"Tell me, about it, Vic," he said, reverting to English as he swung his legs round and sat up to light a cigarette. "For the last day or so she's been acting like she don't want me around. She's started saying things like *'as soon as you get back to Antigua'* and *'you must be missing home'*. I reckon it's time I booked my return ticket," he said, giving me a little grin. Just at that moment I heard the kitchen door slam and Eleanor came into the house from her studio, a large conservatory on the north side of the garden. She exchanged pleasantries with Jelena, our cleaner/housekeeper and then came through to see us.

"Aren't you working today?" she asked me.

"Good morning, Eleanor! I'm fine thank you, how are you?"

"Sarcasm doesn't become you, Victoria," she snapped back at me. "I was simply asking whether or not you'd given yourself a day off, that's all. I thought you had to go out today."

"I had an appointment at the bank which went well, and on the way back I went for a walk round the park as it's such a lovely morning and now I'm going to have a coffee and within minutes will be hard at it once again. I need to talk to you about the interview with the Standard's Art Critic."

"I'll come up to your office in a moment," she said, lifting Tyrone's feet off the sofa and sitting down in their place. "And you can fill me in on what happened at the bank."

"What are you working on? I thought all the work for your exhibition was complete," I said.

"I don't just work for exhibitions, you know that! I'm doing some painting for pleasure. It's a while since I've done that."

"You can do me portrait," Tyrone said.

Eleanor tutted.

"You couldn't afford me!" she snapped back at him. "And are you going to stay in all day today again?"

"Where you want me to go? I don't know no-one except for me old friends and you don't want me to see them. Look how you kicked up last time I went out."

"For God's sake! Do I have to be with you every second of the day? Go for a walk... a jog... to the gym. Can't you go out unless I'm holding your hand?"

She jumped up and strode towards the door, pushing past me in the process.

"Eleanor, what's wrong with you?" I asked. I was surprised to see her like this. Don't get me wrong! She can be moody when she likes and she'd never been afraid to cause a scene, especially since she's become well-known. She can be a right diva. And on the rare occasion she really hasn't liked someone I've seen her be downright unpleasant. But not with Tyrone. Well, not until very recently, that is. Tyrone followed her out into the hallway and caught up with her as she went to go up the stairs.

"Baby, what's up?" he said, catching her arm and spinning her round to face him. She burst into tears and fell into his arms. Leaving them to it I wandered into the kitchen where Jelena was making a batch of dinners for the freezer.

"Hello, luff! You want coffee?" she asked as she looked up from spooning what looked like her scrummy beef goulash into foil containers. Jelena was always smiling and her smile was a great, glorious grin that reached right the way up to her bright blue eyes. Her husband Stan had developed MS in his late twenties, just three years after they'd arrived in Britain and she'd looked after him since, while also bringing up their three children. I often wondered what she had to smile about.

"No thanks, Jelena, I'm just going outside for a moment."

I stepped into the garden and walked down the path towards Eleanor's studio. I don't know why I had the urge to go into it. As her inner sanctum it was a place I rarely visited. But the moment I saw what she was painting her sudden mood swings fell into place. The painting was a coupe d'oeil. Against a backdrop of a Caribbean beach, a large, dark royal palm was reaching from the sand up towards the sky where its leaves opened wide like huge spider legs. But it was only after I studied it for a minute I saw what else it was: the trunk of the palm was an erect penis and the leaves were splashes of sperm ejaculating from it.

And then I knew.

I went back inside the house. Everything was quiet and there was no sign of Eleanor and Tyrone. I climbed the staircase up to my rooms. I took a Diet Coke from the fridge and wandered into my office to start answering the growing list of e-mails in my inbox. After half an hour or so, Eleanor appeared at the door with Tyrone in tow. She came in and sat on the spare chair leaving him standing by the door.

"Darling," she said, looking straight at me and leaning forward to take my hand, "we've got something to tell you."

"I already know," I said. "You're pregnant."

Chapter Six

And so here we all were, just under two weeks later, in a luxury private clinic in Central London; one that was as expensive as it was discreet and one that didn't close for the day because of a Royal Wedding. I looked at Eleanor and Tyrone and closed my eyes again; they hadn't shouted at each other for thirty seconds, which I took to be a good sign. Then Tyrone took a deep breath.

"You're right, Eleanor, this was a mistake, we never expected you to get pregnant, but now you are we have to deal with the situation," Tyrone said.

"And what the fucking hell do you think I'm trying to do here today? I am dealing with the situation in the way we both agreed. Not just me." She pointed at him and then herself several times. "We. You and me. We both agreed on an abortion."

"I went along with what you wanted. But now I've had time to really think about it and I just don't want you to have no abortion. I want you to have my child."

"Well, thank you very much! Lucky old me! Listen, Tyrone, I'm not some sixteen year-old Caribbean *Baby-mommy* who knows no better!"

I shook my head as I thought that that's exactly how she had behaved. No contraception or protection; no thought for the consequences; that was just like an irresponsible sixteen-year-old who knew no better, not a forty-three-year-old who supposedly did. Tyrone sucked his teeth and slowly shook his head while looking at her in disgust.

"I know what this is all about. You think you're a real liberal, innit? An artist, a woman of the world, a free spirit. Someone who does what she likes, when she likes and never gets tired of telling everyone she lives her life her way, on her terms. And being seen around with me? You've loved it. Not just here but in Antigua. You think that letting people see you with a young black dude... people knowing that you're fucking a black guy who could be your son, well, you think that gives you some sort of street-cred or status. Look at Eleanor! She's forty-three but she's got a dude half her age. And a black one. Fuck me! Everyone wants to be her, innit? But bringing up a black kid? Shit no! When we're over and done with you don't want no souvenir like a black kid hanging around, getting in the way, expecting to be brought up the same as your white daughter. That's why you wanna get rid of it."

"You're talking rubbish! Don't insult me with some stupid racism accusation when you know that's not it at all! I'm too old to have another child. My life is good now. I've finally got to where I want to be. I finished bringing up baby years ago. I love my life and the way I live. And there's no room in it for a baby. A baby of any colour."

"Then perhaps you should have thought about that, Mum," I said, unable to keep quiet any longer. "It's like you've just said, you're not sixteen and you're not naive. It's not like you were some young girl he took advantage of. You went into this with your eyes wide open. What would you say if you found out I was having a relationship like that without any protection? You'd call me irresponsible."

I expected her to fly at me but she just slumped into the chair and tears started to pour down her face as she cried silently.

"I know it sounds pathetic," she said, between sobs, "but it wasn't meant to happen." She dived into her Mulberry bag and pulled out some tissues and wiped her face. "I know I was naive and irresponsible," she continued. "I didn't stop to think. I just never ever dreamt I'd get pregnant again, not after all this time, after all these years." She wept silently for a while. "But anyway," she then continued, blowing her nose and suddenly showing signs of her old feistiness again, "why is it all down to me? What about him? Eh? What about you?" She turned on Tyrone with such hatred in her face and voice that he flinched back in the chair away from her.

"I don't remember you offering to use a condom or asking if I was on the pill!" she shouted. I looked at her in disbelief. How could she have ever contemplated having unprotected sex with a man who shagged a different woman every couple of days?

"Well I thought a woman of your age and experience would have had all that sussed. I thought you was probably too old to have a kid. Probably having the menopause or something. How was I to know you was still able to have one?"

"You bastard!" She collapsed back onto the chair again and really started to sob. Tyrone couldn't have hurt her more if he'd tried.

"But, hey! You ain't too old. You're having a kid. My kid and that's cool. Just don't get rid of it. That's all I'm asking. Don't get rid of it. Give it to me. Let me and Mommy take care ah he."

"You've already got a kid you never see. Why do you want this one? You'll change your mind in a couple of months and it'll be abandoned. Left with your mother to bring it up."

"You don't know shit about my other kid, or the situation with her mommy. I don't see her because they live in Virginia. Her mommy's a crazy woman and she just upped and left. I haven't even got their address or a phone number. Nothing I can do about that. But I can do something about this little one."

In spite of my disgust at her lack of responsibility I couldn't fail to feel so sorry for her. This proud, confident, assertive woman had been suddenly reduced to a wreck, a shell of her former self. I actually felt sorry for both of them. I went and knelt beside her and put my arm around her.

"I think you should go home and think about this for a few days," I said. "I understand you don't want to get married and I think that's fair enough. But Tyrone's just offering you another way out. Don't chuck everything away now, just stop and think it all over. For another twenty-four hours if you like."

"I've done nothing but think about it for several weeks now, what good would another twenty-four hours do?" she asked, unconvincingly. She looked as if she might be faltering for a moment, so I pushed on.

"Okay. Look, I know that you're not a normal couple. But what's normal? Perhaps this is a solution that suits everyone. Having the baby and sharing the care with Tyrone."

"We can work something out, Eleanor. We've had a great time together. We're good together you an' me. We've loved each other and now we can love our kid."

"Stop trying to make it into something it wasn't!" She held her hands over her ears to blot out his words, then, turned on Tyrone again. "Love? Love? You're having a laugh! It was never anything more than sex, was it?"

Tyrone was silent. He just looked at her.

"For God's sake, Tyrone, say something! Tell the truth. You know that's all it was. "

Tyrone still didn't reply, he just kept looking at her with a steady gaze. She took a deep breath.

"You are every middle-aged, middle-class white woman's fantasy. Being with you was exciting, something new, something I'd never tried. You are a gorgeous physical specimen. But that's all you were and that's all you are. I might have enjoyed having sex with you for a couple of months but that doesn't mean I was dreaming of marrying you and having your babies. Okay, I admit I did drag you around like a trophy, but I was the envy of every woman that saw us together. And you were happy to play along."

"Me?"

"Yes, you! And you know you got something out of it, too."

"Whoa! Wait a minute, wait a minute. Am I supposed to be grateful or something? Is that what you're saying?"

"Yes, I bloody well am."

Tempers were rising again. I just wanted to be sick. I'd always hated confrontations and this was worse than my worst nightmare. But I was too afraid to leave. I couldn't leave Eleanor on her own. She needed me, even though she didn't seem to know that she did. I turned to Tyrone, silently begging him not to upset her, not to rise to the bait, even though she was being an absolute cow. But he was giving as good as he got.

"Well, you've got a fucking nerve! Grateful for what? For killing my kid? For depriving me of a chance to bring up my own child? Grateful for that?"

"You had a good time with me."

"What? Fucking some old woman?" He sucked his teeth.

"Five minutes ago you were proposing marriage to me!"

"I'll do anything to stop you getting rid of it. Anything! We could do worse than getting married."

"No, we couldn't! And you seem to be forgetting just who started all this. All that *Sweet Lady* stuff. Singing to me on the beach the first afternoon we met. You made the first move. You knew the score."

"I could have had someone young. There was a coupla babes on the beach that afternoon."

"Then why didn't you?"

Tyrone shrugged his shoulders. He had no answer for her. Knowing he'd boxed himself into a corner she wasn't going to let up.

"I'll tell you why. Because picking up older, wealthy women and taking them to bed in the hope they'll pay you for giving them a good time is what you do. You work the beaches, preying on lonely women. You're a hustler! A gigolo! And you got what you wanted out of me, didn't you?"

He held her gaze but didn't answer so she ploughed on.

"We had a business agreement. Yes, it might have been unspoken, but we both knew what it was. I was living out a fantasy. I was getting exciting sex and some fun and some attention. But do you think I believed all the stuff you were saying? Of course not! You've said it to a hundred women before me, but I was happy to go along with it, because I was having a good time. It was all about sex, not some great love story."

"Right! So you was just with me for sex? So what does that make you? A *dutti foot,* innit? An old slapper!"

"You've got some nerve, Tyrone." She gave him a long, hard stare, taken aback by what he'd just called her. "We both used each other. In return for giving me a good time in bed, for letting me parade you around and show you off like a trophy, you got nothing? Is that what you're saying?"

"I ain't saying that..."

"Of course not! Because you know what I'm saying's true. Did you get anything out of having sex with an old slapper? Ummm? Let me see."

Her tone was heavily sarcastic as she counted off the points she was making on her fingers.

"Well, while we were in Antigua you got two months free food and drink; you got a new Blackberry with unlimited credit and a new TV for your mother. I paid off the last instalments on your car, which I later found out you shouldn't even be driving because you haven't got a licence, and I gave you the money for the doors and windows of the house you're supposed to be building. And then you got a free Upper Class trip to England, with free board and lodging, plus a Rolex watch and a gold bracelet for your birthday. And you accepted them all. So what does that make you? Eh?"

He glared at her but said nothing. She gave a sarcastic laugh that sounded dangerously like she was bordering on hysteria.

"You can't even be honest about it!"

"Stop it! Stop it the pair of you!" I said in a stage whisper. "This is a hospital. Keep your voices down! The whole of London doesn't need to know every detail of your relationship." I turned to Eleanor and tried to reason with her. "Eleanor, don't you see? Tyrone's just trying to find another way out. You don't have to marry him. You don't even have to have anything to do with him. All he's asking is to have the chance to take care of his baby. You can't deny him that, can you?"

"You have to give me my child, Eleanor," he said.

"I don't have to do anything."

"Why are you being like this?" I was so confused by all that had gone on and found Eleanor's stance puzzling. But I thought I knew what was behind it all. "It is because of my dad, isn't it? He didn't want to take responsibility for me. He left you alone with me at twenty-one. And now you're punishing Tyrone for that. But he's not my dad and he's not even like him. He does want to take responsibility for his child and you won't let him because of what someone else did to you years ago in different circumstances. How can you deny him the right to bring up his child? Please don't do this for all the wrong reasons."

"This has nothing to do with you, Victoria!"

"Oh, yes it does! That's my brother or sister you're carrying."

"And it's my kid. I must have some rights," Tyrone said.

"This isn't about you having rights and looking after your kid. You don't fool me. This is about fathering a child born here. You think it'll give you the automatic right to stay here, live here, claim benefits..."

"Fuck you!" he shouted at her. "Why the fuck would I wanna stay here for? I can't wait to leave. If I wanted all that I'd just go and stay with my dad again. I just wanna take my child back to Antigua, take care of him and raise him with Mommy. And you're trying to deny me that right, you bitch!"

"Stop it, Tyrone!" I shouted. "Let's go home, wait until tomorrow and then talk about it again sensibly when you've both calmed down a bit."

"I wished I'd kept my big mouth shut," Eleanor said, slowly shaking her head. "I wish I hadn't told either of you about it. I should have just gone ahead and arranged for the abortion without you two knowing anything. I shouldn't have said a word."

She shrugged and shook her head again, angry with herself for her own foolishness.

"Well, my mind's made up," she said. "Just a few more hours and it'll all be over. And we can both get on with our lives. Our very separate lives. I'll get on with preparing for my exhibition and you can go back to the beach and pick up the next old slapper."

Tyrone was distraught. He stood up and smacked his hands against his head. I was taken aback to see tears forming in his eyes.

"I can't believe you're doing this! What do I have to do to stop you? Please, Eleanor. Let's talk about it like Vic says!"

"You can't stop me. My mind's made up and there's nothing more to say."

Just then the door opened and a young woman wearing a pale lilac tunic and trousers, the kind of thing that beauticians usually sport came in. It was obvious from the pinkness of her face that she'd overheard some of the conversation. She gave a false, slashing smile, showing off teeth that were Persil-white and looked at Eleanor.

"Ms West?"

"Yes."

"I'm so sorry to have kept you waiting but we're ready for you now if you'd like to come with me."

"Yes, of course."

The orderly or receptionist, whoever she was, went tactfully back out into the corridor to wait for Eleanor, who reached for her bag. As she did so Tyrone grabbed her arm.

"Don't do this, Eleanor! Please! Don't do it!"

"Let go of my arm!" she said, "Don't cause any more scenes!"

"Do you want me to beg? Eh? Do you?" He fell to his knees in front of her. "Well, look! I'm begging. Okay? I'm begging. I'm begging, Eleanor. I'm begging. Please, don't do this! Let me have my child!" He grabbed her arm again. "Don't go through with it! Let me have my baby!"

Eleanor stared into his face. Slowly she reached for his hand and loosening one finger at a time she removed it from her arm.

"Black dick, Tyrone. That's all you were to me. Just a black dick."

She turned and went through the door leaving the two of us behind in the waiting room.

"I never want to see you again if you do through with this!" I called in vain after her. Like that was going to stop her!

"Eleanor, no!" Tyrone shouted. I put my arms around him as he continued to kneel on the carpet. He buried his head against my belly. "Give me my baby," he sobbed as he clung to me, repeating it over and over again, howling as if his heart would break. At the sight of him my own heart was breaking, too.

Chapter Seven

My heart was in my mouth as I turned the hire car off the main road and started up the dirt track. My mouth, in turn was as dry as a bone and my tongue was stuck to my gums. It wasn't the heat so much as the fact that I was nervous. I looked at the empty plastic bottle of water on the seat next to me. I'd downed it within three minutes of leaving the hotel. Although I had closed all the windows and put the air con on full blast my hands were still sweating as they clasped the steering wheel. I was looking out for a small white house with orange shutters on the right hand side as I bounced along the road, trying to keep the car as steady as possible. That was where the young girl had told me Tyrone now lived. She hadn't been particularly welcoming when I'd called by Mommy's house. Why should she be? She didn't know me; we'd never met. I was just another white tourist looking for him. Probably one in a big, long line. I'd asked for Mommy and she'd told me curtly that she was off-island and went to close the door.

"It's actually Tyrone I'm looking for..." I said.

"He don't live here," she said, eyeing me up and down.

"Could you tell me where he does live?" I asked, trying not to appear too needy or desperate for the information.

"Who wants to know?"

"I'm... er... just a friend. From England."

She laughed out loud.

"Well, I never thought you was a local gyal," she said.

She gave me directions to Tyrone's house and then as I was getting back into the car she stepped out onto the small gallery and called after me.

"What's your name? Who shall I tell him?"

I ignored her, closed the door and started up the car again. I didn't want her to phone him and tell him I was on my way. It wasn't that I wanted to catch him off-guard; I just didn't want to give him the opportunity of going out to avoid me, or of simply not answering the door. Nine months had passed since I'd last seen him and I had no idea what kind of a welcome I'd get from him, especially once I'd said what I had come to say.

Then, as I came round a slight bend in the road I saw the house ahead of me. There was a huge flamboyant tree outside which meant I was able to leave the car in the shade. I closed it up so that it would remain cool, leaving just a tiny gap at the top of the driver's window and taking a deep breath went up the uneven pathway that led to the orange door. There was no bell that I could see so I rapped lightly on the door with my knuckles. There was no reply, so I knocked again, much harder this time. After a few seconds I was rewarded by the sound of shuffling inside.

"Mi a com! Mi a com!" I heard him say. At the sound of his voice my stomach gave a lurch. And then the door opened to reveal Tyrone, as handsome as I remembered him, his hair in a net, wearing a pair of denim cut-offs that revealed the waistband of his boxers beneath. From looking at him I could see that he'd obviously kept up going to the gym since I'd last seen him. The sweet aroma of weed wafted out, like his own particular cologne. And the moment I saw him I knew that I had been wanting to see him again. He looked at me, his eyes widened and then he took a step back almost as if expecting a blow.

"Shit! I mean... Vic! What a surprise!"

"Is it convenient...?"

"For sure! Come in!" He threw the door open wide and stood back to let me in. We gave each other a peck on the cheek as I passed him to then stand awkwardly in the living room.

"Happy New Yea!" he said, laughing nervously.

"Happy New Year!" I replied.

"Take a seat, Vic," he said, indicating the sofa that stood in the middle of the room facing a large, flat-screen TV set and with a lacquered coffee table in front of it. Apart from a table and three chairs against the back wall, they were the room's only furniture. There was also a small, garishly decorated Christmas tree in the far corner, looking as if it was more than ready to be dismantled. He took one of the chairs and placed it diagonally across from me and sat down, looking at me curiously.

"Well, you was the last person I was expecting to see this morning. Or at any time."

"I woke you up didn't I?"

"No! I was awake. Been up ages. I play football on Sundays so I've been up a while. You know, working out some strategies and that." I smiled to myself. Same old Tyrone. Why couldn't he have just agreed that I'd woken him up? After all, it was Sunday morning, most people sleep in if they're not going to church and Tyrone wasn't the church-type in spite of his mother's influence. At least he hadn't been then. Now might be a different story.

"I'm sorry to just turn up like this. I couldn't ring you because I didn't have your number."

"So how did you find me?"

"I remembered where your mum lived from dropping you back there once. I went to the house and the girl who answered the door told me where you lived."

"That's Delia, my sister. She's taking care of the house while Mommy's off-island."

"Is she away for long?" I asked, trying not to sound too interested.

"Maybe. She's with my cousin in New York. Girl had twins and Mommy's gone to take care of them all for a few months or so."

There was an awkward silence as we both chose to completely ignore the elephant in the room.

"So. You here on vacation?"

"Sort of."

"How ya bin?"

"Fine. You?"

"I'm good."

"You look well," I said, truthfully, looking at him and then around the living room. "Looks like things have picked up for you."

"Had a coupla breaks, you know. I'm working a regular job now. A decent job. I got it a few months back, not long after I came home from England. I'm working for a friend of mine who runs his own company. He believed me when I said I wanted to get my life together and he knew I've got IT skills, so he sent me on a bookkeeping course and gave me a chance. And since I've been getting regular money I finally managed to get the house finished," he ended proudly.

"So I see. That's great. I'm well pleased for you."

"Can I get you anything?" he asked, getting to his feel. "I don't drink coffee but I've got some soda or some juice. None of Mommy's ginger beer. Sorry."

"Just some water, please."

He disappeared into a room at the back, which I took to be the kitchen and returned with a glass of water for me.

"So, where you staying? Same house as before in Jolly Harbour?"

"No. Curtain Bluff."

He raised his eyebrows in appreciation.

"Nice one! Were you here for Christmas?"

"No, I just arrived yesterday. I spent Christmas and New Year in London."

"And how long you staying?"

We both burst out laughing at that. It was the opening line of every local man who ever met a female tourist, anywhere in the world.

"I'm not sure yet," I said, still giggling. I guess it was a nervous giggle. "A couple of weeks. I've got a few things to sort out and get straight. Important things." I sneaked an anxious look at my watch and saw that I'd already been here for more than ten minutes.

He looked at me puzzled.

"Whassup, Vic? What's going on? You look like you got something on your mind."

I reached into my handbag and pulled out an envelope with his name written on it in neat, graceful handwriting and gave it to him. He looked at it and then dropped it onto the coffee table as if it had burned his fingers.

"I ain't interested in anything she's got to say."

"I think you'd better read it."

"I've already said I'm not interested. She's out of my life. I've moved on. You can see that."

"Please, Tyrone. Just read it."

"Vic, if you've come here as some sort of peace-making ambassador you've got it all wrong. She can stay in Curtain Bluff and find some other dude to sex her up and drag around. I don't want to see her, I don't want to read her letter, I don't want nothing to do with her."

He curled his legs up onto the chair to sit cross-legged like some sexy, exotic Buddha. I wasn't surprised by his reaction; I knew I was pushing it and with every moment of that day in the clinic as fresh in my mind as if it had been yesterday, I had been expecting this hostile reaction from him. I sighed. This wasn't going to be straightforward. We sat in uneasy silence, the only sound coming from the overly-elaborate gold and cream ceiling fan that was whirring above our heads.

"Okay. Don't read it," I said, dropping the letter on the coffee table. Tyrone stared at it as if it was a loaded gun. "Just give me a moment." I stood up and opened the front door and went down the path to the hire car. As I opened the rear door the cool air from the inside gave me a reassuring welcome. I lifted the front passenger seat forward leaned into the back and peered inside the Moses-basket. The two little eyes, with their beautiful, thick fringe of lashes remained firmly closed. The pink, heart-shaped lips were pursed as if ready to deliver the world's sweetest kiss and the cutest, softest purr was coming from the adorable button nose. I lifted the basket and carried my beloved bundle back into the house. I pushed the door open with my left foot, crossed the living room in three strides that displayed more confidence than I was feeling and placed the Moses-basket on the coffee table. Tyrone, still in his Buddha-pose, froze.

"Here she is! Say hello to your daughter, Tyrone. Say hello to Eliza."

I swear that for at least two minutes he didn't move, didn't even breathe. He just stared at the Moses-basket, his face an undecipherable mask. Then he slowly swivelled his eyes around without moving his head until he was looking at me.

"Is this some sick joke, Vic?"

"No!" I said, shaking my head vigorously. "Of course it's not! She's yours. Yours and Eleanor's. She's five months' old."

"You lie! What's going on here?"

"This is your baby, your daughter."

"Yeah, right! I was there when that bitch got rid of it. Remember?"

I leapt towards him with my fists clenched.

"Don't call her a bitch! Don't you ever call her that in front of me!"

He was taken aback by my reaction and he put his hands up in a gesture of surrender.

"Okay! Okay! But you've changed your tune. I remember all the way home from the clinic you was cussing her like crazy. So just stop playing games and talking in riddles! Do you wanna tell me just what's going on here?"

I backed onto the sofa and sat down. I knew we were in for a long session so I asked him for a drink. He went out into the kitchen and came back with a couple of cans of Coke. He handed me mine and then doing a big detour around the coffee table where Eliza and her Moses-basket were still sitting sweetly, he took up his previous position on the chair. We both popped our cans open and took swigs.

"Well, Eleanor didn't get rid of the baby. That's why I'm here. She didn't have the abortion after all."

"Oh, well that's all right then!" he said, his voice heavy with sarcasm. "So she tells me I'm not good enough to have a baby with, that she don't want my kid; she'd rather kill it. And then what?"

"She came back home the next day to find you and talk things over with you. To tell you she'd changed her mind. When I got back from taking you to Gatwick she was there, waiting for me, surprised that you'd left so quickly."

"What? I was supposed to hang around like some charity case after all that'd gone on that day? After all the things she'd called me? After she'd got rid of my kid?"

"Let me carry on. Let me finish," I said, anxious to get the whole story off my chest. "At first, I was really mad with her. I gave her some more aggro about what she'd done and said. She let me rant on for a few minutes and then said that she'd stayed the night at Max and Gino's. She'd gone to them because she could trust them and she'd told them the whole story. They'd given her tea and sympathy and told her she could stay as long as she wanted. But by the following day she wanted to see you, us, both of us, and explain."

"Oh, what? Her conscience pricked her?"

"No! It wasn't like that?"

"Wasn't it?"

"No! She was genuinely surprised and upset to find you'd left."

"She was? What, was I supposed to stick around for more grief and insults after she'd told me I was a fucking useless waster and that she didn't want me to have the kid?"

I didn't answer. I knew he'd react like this, I hadn't expected anything else, really.

"And now, what? Has she suddenly decided I am good enough to be her kid's dad? Or has she sent you with the kid to warm the waters? Does she expect me to go weak at the knees and then go running down to Curtain Bluff and tell her it's all okay and we're all gonna live happily ever after? This ain't Sister Sister."

"Tyrone! Stop it! That's not it at all!"

"Oh! I get it! She wants to dump it on me then. Me? The bit of rough. Number three on the list. The black dick." He crushed the empty Coke can in his hand and let it drop loudly to the floor.

"Sshh! You'll wake her up!" I said trying to hide my surprise as how he'd remembered word for word all the nasty things she'd said to him so many months earlier.

But he wasn't listening to me. He leapt from the chair in one easy, athletic movement and started pacing up and down.

"Does she think I'm fucking stupid or something? Have I got *MUG* tattooed across my fucking forehead? Eh? No. No, Vic," he said shaking his head, "I've got a life now. I've got a good job, a car, my house's finished. I'm doing good, you know. I don't have to work the beaches no more. That's all behind me. I don't have to pick up no old tourists and leech off them. I got no time for a kid."

"But if your life's sorted out then you can offer Eliza a good life. You wanted her when you were working the beaches. Now you don't do that anymore so you're in a position to really take care of her."

He sucked his teeth and stopped pacing.

"So she does want to dump it on me!"

He disappeared into what I assumed was the bedroom and came back with a half smoked joint, which he lit and inhaled deeply as he sat down again.

"You shouldn't do that, not with Eliza in the room," I said, realising I sounded like some stuffy old-maid.

He shrugged as if he didn't care, but he stood up and went to open a rear door, which seemed to lead to a small veranda.

"That better?" he snapped, glaring at me as he sat down again. He became lost in thought for a couple of minutes. I sat still and waited for him to speak. He moved in the chair and his shoulders sagged a little and he gave a sigh.

"But before, when I was telling Eleanor all this, I had Mommy here. She was gonna help me. Now she's gone. She's gonna be in the States for at least a year, maybe two, or she might never come back. Who knows? She might stay there forever, so she can't help me with no baby." He took another draw on the joint and then shook his head as if he wanted to clear it. "No, Vic. Eleanor had her chance that day in London a year ago and she blew it with balls on. So do me a favour. Pick up the kid, take her back to Curtain Bluff and tell her mommy to take her and to fuck right off!"

"Do me a favour, Tyrone, please. Just read the letter."

He crossed his arms and looked away from me. I gave a mental shake of the head; he was like a petulant little boy. Well, two could play at that game.

"I'm not going anywhere, Tyrone. I'm on holiday, so I've got all the time in the world. I'll sit here all day if I have to. You can go off to play football or whatever else you planned to do with your Sunday and when you come back, I'll still be here, waiting for you to read the letter."

"You can sit here til doomsday. I ain't reading it."

"Okay," I said, grabbing it from the table and slitting it open. "Then I'll read it to you."

He slumped down in the chair, determined not to pay attention. Or, at least, to pretend he wasn't paying attention. Although he sat with his head down and his hands clenched in his lap, I could see he was poised ready to listen to what I was going to read.

"Dear Tyrone. I expect this has come as a bit of surprise to you, or perhaps a shock, more like. But I really do hope it's a pleasant one. Isn't she just the most beautiful little creature you've ever seen? I can see both of us in her and I just can't stop looking at her; so tiny, so perfect. I've called her Eliza. I hope you like that.

Tyrone, I am so very sorry for the way things ended between us and that I wasn't completely honest with you. I was totally confused and messed up by all that was happening to me. And then when I decided to come clean you'd left before I had the chance do so and to put things right between us. Since then I consider myself to have been very fortunate. My exhibition went extremely well and all the paintings were sold which means I've been able to set up a fund for the care of Eliza, and also to arrange for a considerable sum in a legacy for her future once she's eighteen. Victoria has all the details and will accompany you with the documents to whichever solicitor you appoint to take care of these affairs. I would like you to have the painting I was working on when you were in London with me. It's yours to keep or sell, as you wish and it is worth a substantial amount. My agent will arrange its transportation to Antigua, or will sell it in London on your behalf if you just give Victoria your written instructions.

The four months I spent with you were among the best of my entire life. I was absolutely intoxicated by you; by the smell of you, by the touch of your skin, the feel of it under my fingers and of you lying pressed up close on my body, by your huge, dark, almond eyes, by your braids thrashing wildly as we made love time and time again and the sheer wonder and delight of all the pleasure you gave me in and out of bed, by the way you made me feel: like a sexy, sensual, desirable, beautiful WOMAN. I was completely under your spell, drunk and addicted to you and I loved it! You brought me excitement; you turned my life from black and white into glorious Technicolor and for those short four months I really knew that I was alive.

I am so ashamed when I think of the things I said to you. Does it make you feel any better to know that I never did make that bungee jump? I hope so. I stopped at number three; I stopped with you. That said, we both know that we did both use each other to get what we wanted. We were incredibly selfish, but out of our selfishness came this beautiful child.

Take great care of our precious, precious gift. And when she grows up, please tell her that her mother loved her more than she could ever know and every night when she goes to sleep give her a big, loving kiss from me.

I know that you will make something of your life or I would not be sending her to you. You now have someone to work for and strive for – Eliza.

I hope you know that all the insults I threw at you were out of frustration and despair at my situation rather than anger with you. You're in my heart and I think of you now with much love and affection and would not change one moment of our time together.

Eleanor."

I could barely see by the time I reached the end as my eyes were blurred by tears. I wiped the back of my hand across my face and dropped the letter onto the coffee table. Then I looked at Tyrone and was shocked by what I saw. His face was a mask of pure venom. I was afraid to speak.

"She's got some nerve, I'll give her that. She thinks that if she sends me a nice letter a year down the line it'll all be forgiven and forgotten and I'll take the kid off her hands," he spat.

"Tyrone, it's not like that."

"She couldn't even come here herself and show me the baby. Couldn't fucking face me! She sends you as her little messenger. Ashamed and embarrassed at what she said to me! Of course she is!" He picked up the letter and shook it at me. "She calls her baby a precious gift yet she's happy to send her across the world to be raised by a bit of rough like me. By a useless waster! She gave me enough shit about not taking care of my other kid and now she's doing the same. Take the baby back to Curtain Bluff, Vic."

"She's not at Curtain Bluff!"

"Take her back to England, then! Or wherever else Eleanor's fucked off to."

"She's dead, Tyrone."

It took a while for my words to sink in. He stared at me, still breathing heavily from the emotional outpouring of what he'd just said. Slowly, as my words sank in, the expression on his face changed from anger to disbelief. He shook his head.

"No! You lie! You're lying to me, Vic..."

Then he realised from the look on my face that it was true. Eleanor was dead. He let out a long breath.

"Shit!"

He rubbed his hands over his face and exhaled again.

"Vic, I'm so sorry. Shit! How... I mean, what happened?"

"She had cancer. Ovarian cancer."

"But she never said nuttin"

"I know she didn't. As you can probably guess, I knew nothing about it until after she'd come back from Max and Gino's on the day you left. She let me bawl her out and then she told me."

"Shit!"

Chapter Eight

A wave of absolute exhaustion swept over me as I let myself into the house and closed the door behind me, leaning on it to make sure that it was locked tight so that the rest of the world was left outside. The drive back to East London from Gatwick had been horrendous; a crash between a lorry and two cars at Junction 5 had meant sitting in the car for half an hour, engine turned off without going anywhere, before slowly moving again to leave the M25 and drive through what seemed a large section of Kent before we could rejoin the motorway at Junction 4. I had dropped Tyrone off at the South Terminal at quarter past seven and it was now almost half past eleven. He'd jumped out of the car and grabbed his case before giving me a quick peck on the cheek.

"Thanks, Vic. For being on my side," he muttered before disappearing inside the terminal building without as much as a backwards glance at me. And then it hit m that he was going to leave a large hole in my life.

And so then I'd spent four hours on a journey that usually took an hour and a half at most. My head had been spinning; not least of all with worry about Eleanor. I'd prayed that everything had gone well and that she'd got through it without any complications. I was expecting my mobile to ring at any minute with her telling me when to go and collect her. And now, safely back in Whitechapel, I closed my eyes and kicked off my shoes and stood just for a moment enjoying the silence and the sanctuary that home brought.

It was quickly broken by the sound of footsteps running down the stairs.

"Victoria! Where on earth have you been?" Eleanor asked as she got to the bottom. I jolted upright and turned to face her.

"I've been to Gatwick Airport."

"Gatwick Airport?" She looked puzzled, as if I'd said I'd been to the Moon.

"Yes. I gave Tyrone a lift. It was the least I could do. Why? Do you mind? Do you object to me running him to the airport?"

"Well, of course I don't mind! I'm just surprised he's gone."

"Just what did you expect him to do, Eleanor? Was he supposed to come back here and sit and wait for you to see what mood you came home in? To see what else you could do to upset and embarrass him? Wait for you to dig out some more nasty insults? Call him some more disgusting names?"

"Well, no... I just sort of assumed he'd hang around for a while..."

"The same way you just assumed yesterday that he was late because he was up to no good. And the way you assumed he'd go along with what you wanted about the abortion."

"I didn't! Victoria, stop it!"

"No I won't fucking stop it! You behaved like a spoilt little girl, yesterday. You wouldn't even give him a chance! What difference would a day or two have made? Eh?" I was glaring at her, my face just inches from hers, so alike as if it was my own reflection from a futuristic mirror. All my anger and frustration of the last couple of weeks reached boiling point and I was steaming.

"You couldn't even wait a day or two more, to try to talk things over with him properly. Like adults. It was too much to ask that you even tried to see things from his point of view. You were just the same as you always are; it's whatever Eleanor wants Eleanor gets. You had unprotected sex with a guy you just met. One who has a different woman every day and then you were surprised to find out you were pregnant. You *fell* pregnant, like it was some sort of unavoidable accident. You behaved like a stupid schoolgirl!"

"I... I..." She stammered but I wasn't going to let her get a word in edgeways.

"You are not sixteen! You're not some silly little girl who's been conned by her first boyfriend into not using a condom. You're forty-three for God's sake! And how could you not have ever considered you might get pregnant? It's not as if you've had the menopause early, is it? And what about AIDS? You could have caught something terrible from him. You could have put your life in danger. You've behaved like an idiot!" I shouted turning away from her and marching into the kitchen. I filled the kettle with water and slammed it back on its base. I grabbed a mug and spooned instant coffee into it as I became aware of her footsteps coming tentatively into the kitchen behind me. She stood just inside the door, waiting. But I hadn't finished.

"What gives you the right to deny Tyrone the chance to bring up his child? I know you're the mother and you didn't want it, but he did want it! He wanted that kid so badly and you callously went in for the abortion, even though he was begging you not to. He's a broken man. He sobbed all night and looked like he was going to pass out when we got to the airport this morning. I don't know how you can live with yourself," I said, slapping water into the mug and all over the worktop at the same time. It made little sense to me. I felt sick at the thought of Eleanor having Tyrone's baby, but at least if she were it would have been a way of him staying in our lives. I'd tried to deny it, but I knew that deep down inside I had fancied him for a while now. I was like a pathetic schoolgirl with a crush on the dishiest boy in the class; it was nothing more than that. But it was something that I was keeping well and truly to myself. Especially after seeing how eager he had been to get away from me at Gatwick that morning and things were already complicated enough.

"Now that's enough, Victoria!" Eleanor said, grabbing my arm and spinning me round to face her. "I know you're upset about what happened yesterday, but you don't know the half of it."

"And I don't want to!" I snapped back at her. "I've heard all I want to hear."

"I'm still pregnant."

I almost dropped the mug of coffee in surprise. I looked at her, weighing up what she'd said. Could she still be pregnant? I could see that her face showed signs of fatigue and tiredness; there were bags under her eyes and her skin looked sallow, but then again, she'd probably look like that if she'd just had the abortion or any kind of operation. She looked unkempt and she was still wearing yesterday's clothes. Yet there was something about her that made me realise she was telling me the truth.

"How come you're still pregnant then?" I couldn't stop myself from asking.

"I simply couldn't go through with it. Not when it finally came to it. Not after listening to everything that Tyrone had to say. And you. What both of you said really brought home to me that there is precious life growing inside of me. Oh, yes, I've told myself it's just a foetus, it's not a baby, it's just a few cells... But whatever it is at the moment, it's still a new life and in a while it will be a new human being, a new person. One whose father wants it. And I have no right to destroy that person before they've even got started."

"Well, why couldn't you have thought all that before you caused so much aggro and upset?" I wasn't going to give an inch.

"Because it's not that simple!"

"Why not?"

"Because... Look, let's take our coffees into the living room and make ourselves comfortable and I'll explain everything to you," she said. Before I could reply her mobile, which she'd been clutching all the time, rang.

"Hi! Yes, I got home okay, thanks... No... No, he's gone. Victoria took him to Gatwick early this morning apparently... No, I'm with her now. We're just going to have a coffee and I'm going to come clean about the whole thing... Thanks, Max. I'll call you later."

I looked at her puzzled, curious as to what the hell was going on. What did Max know that I didn't and why was he phoning to check up how things were? I poured her a coffee and carried both mugs into the living room. Eleanor was sitting on the sofa and I took the armchair opposite her.

"That was Max. I stayed with him and Gino last night."

I nodded and sipped my coffee. I wanted to hear the whole story, yet part of me didn't want to hear it at all. I was suddenly filled with a sense of dread at what I was about to hear. Eleanor took a mouthful of coffee and put the mug on the carpet next to her. She took a deep breath and turned to face me.

"Do you remember that day in Antigua? It was a couple of weeks or so before we left when I went into St John's by myself one morning?"

I nodded. I remembered it clearly.

"The morning you went to get Tyrone's ticket?"

"Yes, well, I didn't go to get his ticket. I had an appointment with a doctor. An oncologist."

I nearly dropped my coffee. I looked at her in disbelief. And fear.

"I'd had a few problems... for a while but I was unsure... I mean, I'd had pain a couple of times during sex and I felt continually bloated. I was trying to convince myself it was nothing, but I Googled my symptoms and didn't like what came up, so, I made an appointment. They did an ultrasound scan and the doctor said that something was showing up on the ovary that was possibly a cyst but looked like it could be a tumour. They did a blood test, too, and saw that my CA125 reading was high."

"What's that?"

"It's some chemical or protein in the blood that's there all the time but rises when there's cancer in the body. So as you see, the signs weren't looking good."

"But they didn't see the baby when they did all this?"

"No. I probably wasn't pregnant then, but by the time we came home and I followed it up here, I was pregnant and looking at Grade Two ovarian cancer."

I flew to her side and threw my arms around her. She felt small and vulnerable as I held her and I realised just how much weight she had lost. I absolutely hated myself for all I'd said to her and for how I'd judged her. We both clung to each other, sobbing and murmuring "I'm sorry" over and over again, although what she was sorry about I don't know. I was the bitch, I was the nasty cow. Eventually, it could have been five minutes later and it could have been an hour, I let her go and collapsed onto the sofa next to her.

"I should have known," I said. "I should have realised that you had your reasons for wanting an abortion. I should have trusted you and your judgement."

"But if I didn't tell you, you couldn't have known, could you?"

"That's what I don't understand. Why didn't you tell us? Or at least tell me?"

"I didn't want you to know about the cancer until I was recovering," she said, taking my hand. "You do so much for me and you haven't had an easy time of it. I know I'm not the easiest person in the world to live and work with. And I behaved like some sort of Z-list celebrity when I was with Tyrone. I suppose my fling with him was my mid-life crisis. It was a chance to grab some happiness and to kid myself that I'm still young."

"You are still young!! And what are you talking about? I love you, Eleanor. Diva behaviour and all. And how can you say I didn't have an easy time of it? I had the best ever childhood. You made it fun and you loved and took care of me. You were... are the best mum anyone could have wished for."

"Yes, but, I've been difficult sometimes... We've had a bit of a bohemian existence sometimes, I think."

"Shut up! You're an artist, of course you're bohemian! And I've loved our life together. Christ! I had a much better time with you than most kids have with two parents. You know that. So, why, why didn't you tell me?"

"Simply because I didn't want to burden you with it. When you're a mum yourself you'll understand," she said, brushing my hair behind my ear and stroking my face tenderly. "I wanted you to know once I was getting better; when I was well and truly on the road to recovery and then you wouldn't have had to worry so much. But then, finding out I was pregnant was just such a shock. And it made everything so much more complicated. With hindsight I suppose it would have been easier not to tell you or Tyrone that I was having a baby at all and to have just gone and had an abortion and got on with my cancer treatment."

She looked past me, through the panes of the large, bay window and down the garden towards her studio and she became lost in thought for a moment. She smiled and turned back to look at me again.

"I think I was just so overwhelmed by it all that I had to tell someone. And so I told you and Tyrone never dreaming that he'd want me to go ahead with the pregnancy."

"Then why didn't you tell him the real reason why you couldn't?"

"Because... I felt as if I was a failure. Does that make sense? I felt as if by getting cancer I was letting everybody down. That I was weak."

"That's crazy! How can getting cancer be your fault? How does that make you weak? For Christ's sake! You're one of the strongest people I know."

"I know! Saying it out loud sounds stupid and senseless now, but that's just how it was. It was how I felt and I can't help that. Other people feel differently..."

"But if you'd told Tyrone he would have understood. He wouldn't have expected you to carry on and have the baby if you've got cancer."

"Wouldn't he? I don't know."

I bit my lip as I felt it wobbling and tears started to form in my eyes again, but I had to ask the obvious question.

"So, what are you going to do now?"

"I'm going to have the baby."

"No! You can't!"

"I can and I must."

"But, that means you'll be delaying your treatment for, what? another six months at least. You can't afford to do that!"

She shrugged and smiled.

"I've thought a lot about what Tyrone said. Once I'd gone through to have the abortion yesterday morning, I felt a real nagging. His words kept on going round and round in my head and when the orderly gave me the consent form I felt myself hesitating. So I told them I was having second thoughts and needed a couple more days to think about it. The orderly wasn't very happy as you're supposed to have thought about it all before that stage, but I paid a cancellation fee to keep her face straight and said I'd be back in touch. A nurse came and talked to me. She was good and she was very kind. And then the surgeon himself came into the room. I didn't tell them the real reason for my change of heart. I just said I needed another day or so to make up my mind. We agreed that I'd ring them by tomorrow and tell them if I want to go ahead because we're almost at the twelve week period."

"So, have you phoned them?"

"No."

"Well, what's stopping you? Tyrone's gone. He'll never know what happened and he never needs to know. Ring them! Book if for as soon as possible and I'll be there with you all the way through it, no shouting at you or criticising this time, and all through your treatment as well, of course." I lifted her hand to my lips and kissed it. I loved her so much I could feel my heart hurting with pain.

"Tyrone might have gone, but his words are still going round in my head."

"He didn't mean most of that, did he? He said things to hurt you because he wasn't getting his own way. Stop thinking about him and start thinking about yourself."

"But I have to think about the baby, too! And I needed some space when I came out of the clinic yesterday. That's why I went to Max and Gino's. I needed to be able to step back from everything for a while and clear my head. You know what they're like."

I nodded and couldn't help giving a little grin in spite of the shit way I was feeling. Max is Eleanor's hairdresser and Gino is his partner, a solicitor. They live just around the corner from us in a beautiful Victorian house that looks like something out of the pages of Design and Home. Every item of furniture, every rug, every picture, every ornament screams out *style and taste*. And they are the two most loving, caring people I've ever met.

"It was all *'put your feet up, darling'* and *'have a glass of Moet'* but they didn't ask any questions, just accepted that I had a problem I needed to think about. It wasn't until last night over dinner that I told them the whole story. They listened and sympathised and didn't offer any advice other than to come home and discuss it with you and Tyrone. I just didn't imagine he'd have left quite so soon. I hope you sent him home Upper Class, by the way."

I laughed out loud. What a thing for her to think of at a time like this!

"Upper Class was full so he had to slum it in Premium, I'm afraid. But, I want you to tell me what you're going to do now. I want you to phone the clinic and book yourself in for next week. And then I'll come with you to see the oncologist."

"Victoria, you're not listening to me, are you? I've already told you that I'm going ahead. I'm carrying a life inside me. I'm not the only parent on the scene this time. This time the father wants the child and who am I to take that opportunity, that right away from him?"

"But what will happen to you? You can't have any treatment if you're pregnant, can you?"

"No, I can't."

"So you'll die."

"I might. I have to take a chance on that. It's a gamble, but the odds aren't totally against me. Not all cancers are aggressive and hopefully the progression will be very, very slow so that as soon as I've had the baby I can start some treatment."

"But if the progress isn't slow? Then what?"

"Well, we'll just have to wait and see, but I'm betting that I'll be able to have my baby and then start my treatment. I have faith that it's all going to turn out well. For the moment I've made my decision."

I jumped up from the sofa full of rage. My heart was hammering but now it was with anger.

"And what about me?" I screamed. "If something happens to you, what happens to me, Eleanor? Aren't I worth trying to stay alive for?"

Tears were rolling down my face. I was five years old again and my mummy was ill. The thought that she might die, that I might lose her was like a sword ripping me open. She leapt up and put her arms around me, completely enveloping me with her embrace.

"You, my darling, are the only thing that made staying alive worth it more times than you can possibly know."

Chapter Nine

And so, she got on with her pregnancy. But for reasons she wouldn't talk about, refused to contact Tyrone to tell him.

And, of course, things weren't as simple as Eleanor had liked to pretend they were going to be. First of all, her doctors told her that it was highly unlikely she could go full term whether there was any chance of saving her life or not and so they would probably induce her at seven months, or earlier if need be, as long as the baby was ready. This meant the birth would be in September, so it would clash with her exhibition. I was going to have to pull a load of strings and move heaven and earth to get the frigging exhibition brought forward.

The first hurdle was the gallery. The new timescale meant we now needed the exhibition to be shown in late July or early August. I'd had a look on their website and seen this was going to clash with something else they had booked. I went to a meeting with the owners, Jane and Fredrick Butler to try to persuade them to change it for us. Eleanor's pregnancy was still secret; she was keeping right out of the public eye by only leaving the house to see her doctors and they weren't the type to sell their stories to the tabloids. But I knew I had to be honest with Jane and Fredrick, they deserved that from me.

"Come through, darling," Fredrick had trilled leading me into a large office at the rear of their Cork Street gallery that was minimalist and starkly beautiful. "Coffee's on."

Jane rose from a pale pink leather sofa, smiled and held out her hand. We shook hands as we kissed each other on both cheeks and I took a seat beside her. I loved Jane and Fredrick, who were a pair of eccentric poppets and such an unlikely couple. Fredrick was so camp he made Julian Clary look like Sylvester Stallone and Jane, with her short bob that suggested she'd cut it herself and her penchant for tweeds, who resembled a 1940s spinster schoolmarm. Yet they'd been married for thirty-three years and had three strapping sons, none of whom had had the slightest interest in art or working in their parents' gallery and who were a fire-fighter, a maths teacher and an accountant.

Fredrick served me what was probably the best cup of coffee I've ever tasted in a delicate bone china mug and took his seat in the large leather armchair across from us. I decided to wade straight in.

"I'm here to throw myself on your mercy," I said. "We need to bring the date of Eleanor's exhibition forward so that it starts in the last week of July. Now, I know you've got something on then," I continued quickly when I saw the look on their faces, "but there's a serious reason for it. I mean, it's not Eleanor being a prima donna and acting on a whim."

I could see that I had their interest; both of them were looking at me keenly.

"She's pregnant and the baby's due in September."

"Well, that was inconsiderate of her," Fredrick sniffed. "She's known for ages when the exhibition is. She could have planned it a little better. You know, had the baby before or after." Jane gave him a scalding look.

"Sometimes babies come when they think they will and not when you plan," she said reprimanding him. "Look what happened when Edgar was born. We'd been trying for almost three years," she explained to me. "We'd given up any hope of having a second child, really. And then suddenly, I realised I hadn't had a period for three months and that I was pregnant again. And I didn't even have a period after his birth because Sebastian came along just thirteen months after that!"

"Yes, well, darling, I don't think Victoria needs to know all the details of your menstrual history, do you?" Fredrick said.

"The baby's not due until November but she won't be able to go full term," I charged on, wanting to get an answer from them as quickly as I could. "There's a complication."

Jane rose and went across to the desk and sat in front of her MAC. She clicked and scrolled for a moment and then gave a little nod of satisfaction.

"It'll mean we have to cut Eleanor's show by two days because we close for the whole of August for our summer break and we can't alter that because our whole family's joining us at the villa in Capri, but if we do that and bring the whole Jamieson exhibition forward by three days then that shouldn't be a problem."

"As long as Jamieson's people agree," Fredrick said.

"Jamieson is a young artist and we're giving him a huge chance with his first exhibition so he can't be too fussy. And besides, things happen sometimes that can't be avoided." Jane had made up her mind.

"I'm so very, very grateful," I said, feeling as if I was about to start crying, "and I know that Eleanor is, too."

"Well, give her our best," Jane said. "I take it that it's not common knowledge at the moment, about the baby? I mean, we certainly haven't heard anything on the grapevine, and you know how quickly that works!"

"No, it isn't. I suppose it will be soon, but at the moment only a handful of people know."

"Well, nobody will hear it from us!" Jane assured me, while giving Fredrick a *'and they'd better not'* look.

I rose to go and placed the mug on the edge of the desk before giving them both a hug.

"I'll let Rhonda know about the changes and I'll confirm it in writing to you this afternoon." Rhonda was the second hurdle, but I knew from experience that presenting Rhonda with a fait acomplit was the best way of dealing with her. She's a nice enough person and a reasonably good agent, but she's more than a little negative. You know the type: the glass is always nine-tenths empty with no chance of a refill ever. I think she's got a first class honours degree in Putting Obstacles in the Way. If I'd run the idea by her she'd have found a thousand reasons why Fredrick and Jane would never agree. Now, all she had to do was to make a couple of phone calls and rearrange her diary. I sometimes wondered what she really did to earn her twelve and a half per cent.

"We'll have to change all the press and publicity stuff to show the new dates. And, of course, tell his agent that we'll pay for Jamieson's changes, too. And for all your costs," I added.

"Fredrick will get right on the phone now and start things moving from here," Jane said, beaming at both of us.

"Yes, dear, no dear, three bags full, dear!" Fredrick said as I left the office.

To the casual observer, Eleanor seemed to bloom in pregnancy. Her skin and hair were glowing as if she'd been on some sort of fabulous detox diet, but I could see just how much weight she was losing. She favoured billowing kaftans, rejecting the modern trend for not wearing maternity clothes as "ghastly".

"I've never seen anything more revolting in my life than these Chavs who wear tight vests with their huge bellies showing. Disgusting!" was her view on it.

But as her belly grew, the rest of her body seemed to shrink. She'd never been particularly robust and now she was just belly and eyes; a distorted lollipop. The press now knew she was pregnant, but Rhonda had issued a statement asking for *"privacy at this very private time"*.

The exhibition was a huge success and even though the news of her illness hadn't been released, every painting was sold by the second day.

"If they all realised these might be the last paintings I'll ever do they'd see just what wonderful bargains and investments they've got," she chuckled.

She enchanted everyone when she put in a short appearance at the exhibition - buyers, critics, the general public alike. She'd taken special care over her appearance. Her make-up and hair were immaculate thanks to Max and she looked stunningly, hauntingly beautiful. But she was becoming increasingly exhausted as the cancer began to tighten its lethal grip. By mid August her gynaecologist and her oncologist agreed that the baby had to be induced as soon as possible. Eleanor had begun to complain of migraines and her moods became erratic; she'd go from the depths of despair to being life-and-soul of the party. The cancer had spread to her lymphatic system and a secondary tumour was discovered in her liver. This didn't just mean that things looked grim for her, but for the baby, too. Various tests were carried out and on 20th August Eliza was born at just under 30 weeks by Caesarean section, weighing just 3lbs.

She was put into intensive care and Eleanor insisted on being wheeled down to see her at every opportunity. She was like a tiny little doll and I found seeing her with so many tubes attached was really upsetting. I can't imagine what it must have been like for Eleanor to look at her but actually seeing Eleanor was even more upsetting.

A week after the birth I sat next to her bed in the luxurious room in the private clinic as the warm afternoon sunshine streamed through the window and held her hand. I'd wanted to take her home but she wanted to be near Eliza who was still far too weak to come out of hospital and I understood that. She squeezed my hand and gave me a wry little smile.

"Well, I never was much of a gambler, was I?" she said, her thumb stroking my knuckles. "I really did believe that Lady Luck was on my side and that I was going to be able to give birth to Eliza before the cancer took a hold."

"There's still a chance for you," I said, knowing full well that there wasn't. "Now you're no longer pregnant you can start your treatment."

"Oh, darling! You know as well as I do that it's too late for any treatment now. I'm too weak to take it and the cancer's too far advanced to respond to anything."

"No!" I said, tears yet again springing to my eyes, "We have to try..."

"Don't, Victoria! It is far too late, my darling girl. I know what the situation is. Do you think I haven't looked at myself in the mirror? Do you think I can't see what's happening to me? And the pain's only bearable because I'm on this," she indicated an IV that was going into her thigh. "I can actually feel how my body's breaking down."

"So are you giving up?" I knew she was speaking the truth but I didn't want to hear it. I wasn't ready to lose her, however selfish that was.

"I never give up, you know that. But I feel like shit. I'm trying to stay positive but I'm angry that there's nothing I can do and I know you're angry with me, too. I'm so, so angry with myself. But how could I have sacrificed our little Eliza? I took a gamble that I could have her and still have time to get well. Well, now I've found out the hard way I couldn't; my gamble didn't pay off. But I don't regret going ahead and having her. How could I? I'm just so sad about so many other things, like not seeing her grow up and not being here for you."

"What's the point in having her if you knew you wouldn't live to see her grow up? Who's going to take care of her now? Me? I'm going to be stuck with a baby, Eleanor. How fair is that?"

As soon as I'd said the words I wanted to grab hold of my tongue and cut it out. Yes, I was angry that Eleanor was dying; angry that she was going and leaving me because she'd been all I'd ever known and I loved her more than I could possibly tell her or make her realise. And now I was going to be alone to bring up this baby, the reason why she'd sacrificed herself and given up her life was going to be left to my care. But Eleanor was dying.

"Please, Victoria, don't take it out on Eliza! She's the innocent in all of this. And I know you are, too. All I'm asking is that you look after her for a couple of months and then you take her to Antigua, to her father."

My chin hit the floor. I couldn't believe what I'd just heard.

"You want Tyrone to bring her up? After all you said about him?"

"Yes, I do," she nodded.

"But you've refused to even tell him about her up until now!" I said my frustration showing.

"That was because I thought I'd get through this. I thought his presence during the pregnancy would bring stress that I didn't need and I certainly didn't want his pity! But now... Well I think he should be given a chance. I've done what he asked. I've given birth to his daughter and now I'm giving her to him, to give him a chance to turn his life around and work hard and take care of her."

"And what if he doesn't?"

"Are you changing your mind? Weren't you the one sticking up for him, telling me he should be given a chance? Now, suddenly, you're not sure any more?"

"Well, I... I just thought you needed time to think about it. I thought the idea was that you'd bring the baby up between the two of you."

"It was!" Her voice was tense with irritation at my lack of understanding. "But it hasn't turned out that way, has it? " She leaned across and picked up an envelope from the bedside table and placed it in my hand. "This is for Tyrone. I want you to give it to him when you take the baby to him. I've made provision for you, Victoria. I know it won't be easy for you to look after Eliza on your own so there's money enough for a nanny until you think the time's right to take her to Antigua. I'm bequeathing the palm tree painting to Tyrone. It should bring more than enough money to take care of him and Eliza for a long time, especially once I've gone. All my work, every painting I've ever done will be worth so much more then," she said wistfully.

How could I deny her what she was asking? She was dying. I was losing my mother; my rock, my comfort, my strength. But I was still alive and she was dying. I clutched her hand tighter, laid my head on the pillow and pressed my cheek against hers.

"Of course I will, Eleanor. I'll do whatever you want."

"I love you so much, Victoria. My life would have been so empty without you. Please,,, forgive me for all that I've done wrong..."

"You've done nothing wrong! Nothing!" I kissed her cheek and then laid my head back against it, snuggling up tightly to her. "I love you, Mum."

An hour later she died.

Chapter Ten

Tyrone patted my arm. Tears had formed rivulets down his face and soaked his chest. I could tell he wanted to comfort me but he was unsure what to do. He wiped the back of his hand across his face and took a deep breath, exhaling it noisily and shook his head.

"You've made me feel like a right shit. Why the fuck didn't she tell me she had cancer?"

"Did you listen to what I just said? She hadn't told anyone. And that's what she was coming back home to do, to tell us, but you'd already left to come back here."

"But she could've called me! She could've come out here or sent you!"

"I don't know why she didn't! Do you think I haven't asked myself all these questions a thousand times? I did suggest it once - that she should phone you - but she thought you'd tell her to fuck off so she never did. And she made me promise that I wouldn't phone you either. Then as time went by well, then it became more and more difficult to contact you and then there came a moment when she was never going to do it. She simply said you'd be an added complication to the pregnancy; she didn't need any more stress. And I suppose she'd gone through one pregnancy alone so she thought she could go through another. And besides, she had me there."

"I should've stayed in London and not run off like that. But I was angry at how she'd spoken to me and humiliated me. And how she'd refused point blank to even think it all over. I mean, how was I supposed to know she'd change her mind? She was so determined.

How was I supposed to know she was ill? I'm not a fucking mind-reader..." His voice petered out.

"Well, you didn't know, I didn't know, nobody knew. But you do know now."

"Yeah, okay, so I know. But that doesn't mean that I can do what she wants."

"Well, you've changed your tune!" I was beginning to get angry with him. "What happened to all that *'I'm gonna take care of my kid'* stuff? Was that all just a load of bollocks? Just a bit of bravado?"

"No! Course it wasn't! I'm just confused. I wasn't expecting this, innit? It's been a shock."

"It was a shock for me, as well. And I've lost my mum on top of everything else. I've done what she asked, I've looked after Eliza until now, but I can't carry on indefinitely. I need you to take responsibility for her."

"I can't!"

"Yes you can! Stop feeling sorry for yourself! You're not the first man to discover he's a father, for fuck's sake!"

"But I've got a life now!"

I jumped up and clenched my fists but kept my hands at my sides as I couldn't trust myself not to smack him on the nose. I was almost blind with rage at his words and his self-centred attitude.

"You selfish pig! That's what Eleanor said, if you remember. She had a fabulous life but you seemed to think that wasn't a valid argument when it suited you."

"I need to work. I need money and my job. What can I do with a baby?"

"I thought you wanted to take responsibility for your child."

"I did! I do!"

"You said you wanted the chance to be a good dad."

"I know I said that. But things have changed."

"Yes! They have! They've changed for the better! Before you were just a beach bum, now you've got a good job and a future!"

"But Mommy's not here to help me! Can't you understand that, Vic?"

He slumped forward with his head in his hands, groaning. I didn't say a word. I wasn't going to make it any easier for him because I was, quite frankly, more than upset and angry with him and his attitude. After a couple of moments he slowly raised his head and looked at me.

"I know what you're thinking."

"Do you?"

"Yeah. You're thinking I'm a right arsehole, innit?"

I shrugged as I felt some of my anger dissolve. I was finding it hard to stay mad at him, but I still nodded my head in agreement.

"Let's say, I'm a bit disappointed in your attitude. After all, Eleanor's even supplying the money for you to provide a decent, loving home for Eliza. Neither of you will want for anything. If you can't manage you can pay for a nanny and you can even send her to school in England when she's older if you want to. And once she's grown up she'll have her own money from her trust fund."

"What money's Eleanor giving me?" He'd been so knocked sideways by the morning's events that he obviously hadn't taken in half of what I'd said to him.

"The palm tree painting. She said you can do what you like with it. You can keep it or you can sell it if you want to. It's yours after all."

"One painting? Like that's gonna raise enough money to take care of a baby!"

"Tyrone! I don't think you realise just how well-known or talented my mother was," I scolded him. "The painting could be worth perhaps half a million pounds. Especially now that she'll never produce another picture again." I pulled a figure out of the air; I had no idea of the exact value but I knew it would be at least six figures. That was a real fortune in Eastern Caribbean Dollars; in any currency. "If you wait a couple of years before you sell it, it'll be worth a lot more."

He nearly fell of the sofa.

"That's... well that's... fucking hell!"

Then he looked at me quickly, afraid I might be joking or that he'd misunderstood me.

"I mean, that does make it easier for me to raise her well. Knowing that everything's taken care of, you know what I'm saying? If I've got no financial worries then I can give her a good life."

"Right! You've finally got it! That was Eleanor's intention. Of course, you have to realise that it might take a long time to arrange an auction and for you to get the money through. It'll be a few months at least. And Eliza's going to need good care taken of her until then."

He leaned back against the cushions, his eyes closed, lost in thought for a few moments. Then he opened his eyes and sat up and turned towards me.

"I don't want you to think that I'm some kinda mercenary, but knowing that money ain't gonna be a problem shines a different light on things. So, could we, maybe, you know, work something out between us? You know, like you staying here with her 'til then?"

"You mean you want me to be the unpaid nanny until you get your money?" I asked him, incredulously.

"Not, exactly that!" he said quickly. He sat up and took my hand. "But, if you took an apartment and looked after her for a while I could come by and see her every day..."

"Wait a minute!" I said, snatching my hand away from his. "You're not getting away with being a part-time father. How about Eliza living here with you and me dropping by to visit her? Eh? Don't forget, Tyrone, that I've got a life, as well. Back in England. I've already put everything on hold for the last six months to look after your daughter! I don't think you quite appreciate what I've been through." I spat the words at him.

He sat there, big eyes looking at me like some dejected puppy, waiting for me to say something slightly more encouraging. I felt sorry for myself and I felt sorry for him. Most of all I felt sorry for my little sister, Eliza, whom it seemed like nobody wanted to take care of on a permanent basis. I could feel myself weakening. After all, I loved little Eliza and saying goodbye and leaving her behind in

Antigua was going to be very hard. Perhaps I'd feel better if I could do it gradually. And I had to admit that seeing Tyrone again had stirred up all the feelings I'd had for him. He was as gorgeous as I'd remembered him and I liked the idea of being close to him for a while longer.

"Look! I'm not promising anything long term, but I can stay for a couple of weeks to help you out until you get settled into a life with her and you've sorted out how you're going to take care of her."

"You'd do that?" He sat forward eagerly and took my hand again. I just loved the touch of his skin. "It'd be great if you would. You know, just for a while..."

"Tyrone, Eleanor's dead. But little Eliza's alive. None of this is her fault."

I took my hand from his and stood up and crossed to the Moses-basket where Eliza was still sleeping sweetly, her little fists clenched either side of her face, her eyelashes two black-edged half-moons either side of her nose.

"Here is the baby that you so wanted. Here she is. Don't you even want to look at her?"

He slowly got to his feet and leaned forward and looked into the little crib. I saw his face soften as he saw his daughter properly for the first time. I lifted Eliza up and held her towards him.

"Tyrone: meet Eliza."

I put the baby into his arms and took a step back. He stared at her in awe and wonderment as if he'd never seen anything as beautiful or as special.

"Do... do you think she looks like me?" he asked after a moment.

I was so full of emotion at seeing his reaction that I could barely speak so I nodded my head furiously until I could trust myself to reply without getting emotional.

"Yes. She's gorgeous," I finally managed to say.

He held Eliza in front of him, looking into her face and smiling. Then he slowly lowered himself back onto the sofa and spent the next hour gently rocking her up and down using his knees to balance her, his eyes bright with loving tears. The lump in my throat felt like a jagged rock as I watched the two of them together. Neither of us said a word until Eliza woke up an hour later with a howl to let us know that it was lunchtime.

Chapter Eleven

And so that's how it began, our strange little family unit. We agreed that we both needed to be with Eliza for the time being. She was, after all, used to me and knew me, whereas she didn't know Tyrone and it seemed wrong to me to just dump her with him and I didn't want to do that. Although I needn't have worried; it had been love at first sight for Eliza, as well as Tyrone. When she'd stopped wailing for her lunch and had greedily gulped down a bottle that he had given her, her eyes searching his face, never leaving it and her fingers wrapped around his thumb the whole time, she then gave him her biggest and best smile followed by a gurgling chuckle, a huge burp and was promptly sick on his shoulder and down his back.

"Welcome to fatherhood," I said. And he'd beamed back at me.

Tyrone's little house only had one bedroom, which he gave up to me saying that he'd sleep on the sofa, which pulled out into a bed. I'd thought about renting a house and visiting every day but that just added an unnecessary complication we could do without as I needed to be as hands-on and as near to Eliza as possible. The easiest solution was for Eliza and me to move in with Tyrone. I'd suggested he should rent a bigger place, one with two bedrooms, but he was proud of his home and said that we could manage as it wasn't going to be long term, just for a short while.

"I know that Potters ain't exactly Crosbies, but it's fine for now. Later on I'm gonna get a piece of land and build a house fit for my little princess to grow up in!" he boasted, shaking his head at her and tickling her belly. She giggled happily in reply as if she'd understood what he'd said.

"I don't want to keep mentioning money," he'd said on that first night after Eliza was settled and sleeping soundly, "because I don't want you to take things wrong, but, you know, like realistically, how long do you think it'll take to sell this painting and for me to get the money? I mean, not for me, not because I want it for myself, but so that I can make things nice for Eliza."

"It might take a while, yet. Probate was granted just before Christmas so the painting can be released to you as soon as we do the paperwork, but if you're going to sell it then that'll take quite a while to organise."

"I'm only selling it for Eliza!" he shot at me.

"I know you are. What're you snapping at me for?"

"I just don't want you, or anyone, thinking that I don't appreciate the painting or nothing."

"Of course they won't. What would you do with it if you held onto it? Hang it up in here? It'd take up the whole wall. And besides, you'd probably never get insurance for it just to hang in your home." I smiled to take the sting out of my words as I looked around the sparsely-furnished living-room. He was so proud of what he'd achieved yet so vulnerable and touchy about everything that he saw offence where none was meant.

"Eleanor left it to you so that you could sell it and raise some funds to finance Eliza's upbringing. She said that much in the letter."

"Yeah, well, just so's we're clear. I don't want you thinking that I'm taking your inheritance or nothing."

"Stop being so touchy! Eleanor was her own person, she left you the painting. And besides, she's not exactly left me penniless. I won't be contesting the will or trying to seize the picture from you, don't worry."

He sniffed in agreement and nodded his head.

"But what we do have to sort out are the finances in the meantime," I said. "Eliza needs things, like a cot. She can't sleep in the Moses-basket every night. She's still in it because she's so small for her age but she's fast outgrowing it and she needs to be sleeping in a cot."

"We can go to Shoul's or Town House Furnishings tomorrow and get one. How much do they cost?"

"I've no idea how much they are here, but taking care of her won't come cheap. It's not just a cot; you're going to need money for baby formula and Pampers and clothes and all kinds of things. I don't know what you think about this but, what I was thinking was, that I open up an Eliza Fund to buy things like a cot and clothes and everything she's going to need and then once you've got your money through from the painting you can pay me back."

He put his head on one side, squinted a little and looked at me for a long time.

"You'd trust me to do that?" he asked. "I mean, you're sure you're happy doing it? Cos I don't want no recrimination, you know what I mean? I don't want you to start saying that I owe you this and I owe you that and that you're paying for everything and I ain't paying for nothing."

"Tyrone! Shut up!" I said. "You know I wouldn't say that!"

"But do I, though? I mean, I hope you wouldn't but things get complicated and lines get blurred when money's involved."

"Well, if we don't do that, how will you pay for everything that Eliza needs?"

"Well, that's true. Look, I know you're right and I'm sorry," he said, looking contrite. "I'm just still a bit uncomfortable... about the beach-bum thing, you know."

"I know you are. And I'm sorry about that. Look, let's clear the air, shall we? I'm sorry for not liking you to start with, but I hope you saw at least by the time we got to London, that I was your friend. Am your friend! The stuff you used to do when you met Eleanor, well, you don't do it anymore. That's behind you now, isn't it? I can see you've changed. You've moved on and your life is better. You're not relying on anyone but yourself."

He nodded his head and cracked his fingers.

"Too right! I'm a different person now. I'm making something of my life."

"Of course you are! But you need help with buying stuff. Babies are expensive creatures. After we get the cot there's still a push chair, a car seat, a play pen..."

"And she's gonna have the best of everything. We're not gonna get her anything cheap, you know. I'll get Mommy to buy stuff in New York and ship it down for us. My little girl's not gonna want for nothing!"

He stood up and crossed to the Moses-basket and peered inside for the tenth time in as many minutes, grinning like he'd just been told he'd won the lottery. Perhaps he felt as if he had; he was happy with a capital H. He reached inside and with his finger gently stroked her little cheek.

It was the most loving, tender thing I'd ever seen.

"And we have to have a baptism. That's important," he said, looking at me defiantly as if I was going to argue with him. "We have to make sure that we introduce her to Jesus. And I'm gonna take her to church and make sure she grows up to be a good girl. One that makes her Daddy proud. Not one of these girls that's drinking and dressing provocatively at fourteen and looking for men," he said, sucking his teeth.

"I'm sure she'll make him very proud whether she goes to church or not."

"But going church is our way here in the West Indies. Everybody goes church."

"That's fine, Tyrone, it's your choice to make." I didn't say that I'd never known him to go to church. "As her father you decide what she does until she's old enough to make her own decisions."

"Shit! That's some responsibility!" he said, beaming with the thought of it.

Chapter Twelve

We soon settled into a pattern. Tyrone went to work each day, Monday to Friday and I took care of Eliza. Then in the evenings, after he'd showered and changed and eaten his dinner he would do the night shift while I either got on with my own work of administering Eleanor's estate, or I went out for a while. At the weekend we shared looking after her; sometimes me, sometimes Tyrone and sometimes we were all together, the three of us. Those were the times that I loved best of all. I could pretend that we were a real family; a couple with their child. A lot of people took me for Eliza's mother. I never bothered to correct them as it seemed a strange set-up to anyone other than Tyrone and me.

I was able to sort out most things to do with Eleanor's estate, which was becoming worth more and more with each passing day, via e-mails or through Skype calls, although with the time difference with London of five hours I often found myself talking to Rhonda at four or five am. Still, at least I was able to do it and for that I was grateful. Thank God for technology!

The sale of Tyrone's painting, which Eleanor had named *Erect Royal Palm,* was set for October through Sotheby's London. It was to form part of their auction of works by late twentieth and early twenty-first century artists. Rhonda said there had been a rush of interest in it, which was very promising for Tyrone and little Eliza's futures. It also looked as if I was going to be in Antigua until at least then which I was secretly delighted at.

I'd actually begun to have a life of my own on the island, which surprised me. I'd made some friends down in English Harbour, Rose and her husband Graham, who ran a small property business and Fiona, a holiday rep who'd stayed on and lived with an Antiguan who repaired boats, and once or twice a week I'd drive down and have dinner with one or other of them at Jonny Coconat's or one of the other restaurants in the area, or they would come up and meet me in St John's. I'd also started going to an Open Mic night, which was held twice a month in Heritage Quay, where local writers gathered and performed their work. I wasn't a writer, but I loved listening to them, even though I sometimes didn't understand everything when a poem was in dialect. It also meant that I'd made some Antiguan friends who were people I had a lot in common with and I really enjoyed these sessions. But the evenings I enjoyed most were those spent at home, sitting with Tyrone, chatting, eating together and watching TV. I saw what he was; a decent, good man who loved his daughter to distraction and took great pride in her and in his home. He'd dropped the mouthy beach boy and Essex street kid personas and was now simply being himself. He was great company, an articulate, well-mannered, funny, considerate man and I knew that my being in lust had turned to being in love. Yet he kept his distance from me, always behaved totally correctly around me and treated me like his sister. He couldn't possibly have guessed how I felt and there was no way I was going to let him know.

And to my great delight, Megan had been back in Antigua, too. I'd looked for her as soon as I'd arrived back in January, knowing that she'd be staying in Jolly Harbour as usual. She'd almost hit the floor when she saw me and Eliza.

"Why didn't you come for New Year's Eve? We had a blast. I think I'm still hung-over!" she giggled, taking the Moses-basket from me and pulling me inside.

We sat on the terrace of her parents' house in Jolly Harbour, drinking rum punches while I told her the whole story.

"Holy shit! So that makes Tyrone your step-daddy!"

"No it doesn't! He's not related to me at all!

"He's your half-sister's father, so that makes him your half-father," she screeched.

"Megan, there is no such relationship," I scolded her.

"There is now!" she said, laughing her head off.

Unfortunately, she was leaving the following day, so I hadn't been able to see her again after I'd been to face Tyrone and introduce him to Eliza. But she'd phoned me from the airport as she was waiting to board the plane.

"I couldn't wait until I got home and you got round to sending me an e-mail. So what did he say?" she asked.

I told her a very brief version of what had happened and how we planned to deal with the situation.

"Eeeekkk!" she screamed. "You're gonna be living with Tyrone?"

"Not living with as in *living with*," I said. "You know what I mean."

"Well, it won't stay plutonic for long!" she said. "I'll put money on the two of you getting together!"

"Oh shut up!"

She'd squealed again and then said she had to go as the flight was being called. She came back to Antigua at Easter and we'd spent lots of time together and she'd fallen into the pattern of coming to Potters and hanging out with Tyrone and me most nights. We all got on well, it was easy company. We'd eat a simple supper and then sit and talk and drink rum punches, while Tyrone joined in and occasionally smoked some weed. That was the only time I allowed him to smoke, in the evenings when Eliza was safely in bed asleep. And he didn't argue. In fact, he was smoking less and less, which I liked. We also seemed to have a *no-visitors* rule, too. If either of us had the chance, the opportunity or the need for sex, then we'd conduct our business away from the home, away from Eliza. Neither of us wanted anything to taint that little girl's life, although in all that time I'd only had a two-night fling with an American who'd been on a boat that was island-hopping. His name was Chris and I'd met him in Abracadabra in English Harbour one night. It had been okay sex that had fulfilled a need. He'd been good fun and I'd enjoyed myself with him but neither of us felt the desire to take the other's e-mail address or keep in contact. Once he'd sailed out of Falmouth Harbour, he'd sailed out of my life. I wasn't bothered. I hadn't liked him that much and I have to confess that all the time we were doing it I was imagining that it was Tyrone I was with.

Megan was put out to hear that she'd lost her bet so far.

"You are kidding me!" she screeched. "You're living in the same house and he hasn't made a move on you yet?"

"Why would he? He doesn't see me that way."

"He's a virile young guy and you're a hot babe. I am amazed!" she said.

But sometimes I looked at the way she looked at Tyrone and the semi-flirtatious way she spoke to him and thought that she fancied him herself.

"You're forgetting that he's got a woman," I said, hoping the disappointment didn't show in my voice.

Tyrone's girl-friend, Monique, was a local woman who didn't really like me and who couldn't get her head round our relationship and like Megan, was sure that the two of us were secret lovers. She was glamorous in a very extrovert way. By day she worked in a law office and wore sedate suits with high necked blouses. Out of work she dressed to kill: tight-fitting, low-cut tops and tight jeans that showed off a shapely bottom that you could have balanced a mug on. Her face was beautiful, but she ruined her looks by always scowling. At least whenever I saw her she was scowling. She often came by the house, usually unexpected and uninvited. I was sure she did it in the perverse hope that she'd find the two of us in bed together or having wild sex on the back veranda. She was, of course, always disappointed. Her attitude to me was somewhat erratic; occasionally she'd be all over me, sometimes even smiling, being nice and treating me like I was her new best friend but most of the time she'd barely acknowledge me, suck her teeth and toss her head as if I was beneath contempt. And she always spoke to Tyrone in dialect and sometimes she even used it to me, laughing out loud when I couldn't understand to rub in the fact that I was an outsider who didn't fit in at all.

"You might like to tell Monique she's got nothing to fear from me," I said to Tyrone one day after a particularly tense visit. "No, don't deny it!" I said, seeing that he was about to. "Don't say you don't know what I'm talking about! She was so rude to me tonight and I'm not going to be spoken to or treated like that again."

"What she say?"

"She made a comment about foreign women who come here and take the men."

"When she's talking about foreigners, she ain't talking about you. She's talking about the Jamaicans and Guyanese. You know the set up. Antiguan women don't like them. She don't mean you."

"Well, it feels like she does! And I know it's because she thinks there's something going on between us; you and me." I felt myself blush as I said it.

"I've told her a thousand times that we're just friends. I told her you're not a woman I'd take for sex."

"Oh, thank you!"

"I don't mean it like that! I just mean that we're like family. I'm Eliza's daddy, you're her sister. But sometimes Monique don't see it that way, you know what I mean? She's jealous and possessive. She does my head in most of the time."

"Then why do you stay with her?" I blurted out. He looked at me for a few seconds without saying anything, and then he smiled.

"Why do you think?" he said. "A man's gotta do what a man's gotta do!" he added, laughing his head off. I felt as if he'd stabbed me in the heart.

One morning in early July I was sitting on the veranda reading, enjoying a rare half an hour to myself while Eliza took her morning nap. She was ten months old now, and becoming a real handful. She was crawling at high speed all over the house and was almost able to pull herself up to stand upright. Mommy had sent a beautiful baby walker from New York which Eliza loved using. Unfortunately she mistook the living-room for Brands Hatch and would go zooming around knocking into everything and screaming out with laughter as she went. She was a happy little soul, but she demanded a lot of attention. Yet with her father it was a different story. She was at her happiest sitting on Tyrone's lap, snuggled against him while we sat and chatted. She'd pat her hand against his chest or his face and smile contentedly. I sometimes think that Tyrone thought I was exaggerating when I said she'd been naughty or had given me the run-around all day. For Daddy she was a good girl, always.

I was brought out of the book I'd lost myself in by the beep of my phone. I picked it up and saw a text from Megan:

Hi babe! Great news! Comin 2 c u 4 carnival! Can't wait arrivin 07/28 ticket booked. Luv ya! ☺ ☺

I gave a great big smile to myself and sent a text back saying I couldn't wait either and was looking forward to seeing her, too. I'd been a bit apprehensive about Carnival; I wasn't sure if it was going to be my thing with all the drinking and partying, not to mention the beauty pageants and calypso contests, but with Megan here I knew I'd have a good time whatever we did.

When Tyrone got home that evening I was eager to tell him about Megan's visit.

"Yeah, good news, huh?" he said, unsurprised.

"How did you know she's coming?"

"Well, er, she sent me an e-mail."

"When?"

"Yesterday."

"And you didn't tell me?"

"She said she wanted to tell you herself. Didn't want me to spoil the surprise."

"So what are the two of you e-mailing about?"

"Nothing!"

"Nothing? You must e-mail about something!"

"Christ! What is this? The Spanish Inquisition?" he marched off into the bathroom, leaving me to think about it. When he came out he was all smiles, as if he hadn't snapped at me.

"What's for dinner?" he asked.

"Chicken," I said, walking past him into the kitchen.

"Hey, Vic! Don't be like that! Megan and I sometimes exchange e-mails, you know, silly little things, chain letters, that sort of thing. And yesterday I commented on one of her Facebook posts and she messaged me to say she'd booked her ticket but not to tell you because she wanted to tell you herself. What's the harm in that?"

Now I felt really stupid. I'd behaved as if I was six and my best friend had shared her sweets with someone else.

"Sorry!" I said.

"No problem. It'll be great for you to have your friend here for Carnival. You can lime together and have a good time. You'll love it. Everyone loves Carnival."

The days until Megan's visit seemed to go slowly, but then suddenly, she was arriving I was at VC Bird to pick her up.

"Vic!" she screamed and came running towards me on six inch heels, a porter struggling behind her with enough luggage on his trolley to match Cheryl Cole on a world tour.

"Where's Eliza?" she asked looking round, surprised to see me on my own I suppose.

"At home with Daddy! Big sister's having the afternoon off!" I said, linking arms with her as we walked to the far end by the Virgin Check-In area where I'd illegally left the car for five minutes, having a bet with myself that I'd be back at the car before the airport police were on the scene.

I enjoyed our drive down the west coast to Jolly Harbour as I didn't go that way very often now, and Megan was a great companion.

"So, tell me all about life in Potters!" she said as we drove past the Antigua Athletic Club on our way out of the airport. "What's been happening?"

"Same old, really, just like it was when you came at Easter. You know, I look after Eliza during the day and Tyrone does the night shift and then at weekends we share the care."

"Monique still on the scene?"

"Yes, unfortunately. She clings onto him like a barnacle on a boat. And she's still as rude as ever to me. She takes a half-hearted interest in Eliza sometimes, but even she doesn't like her! She screams if Monique tries to pick her up!" I laughed and Megan joined in, liking the idea of Eliza rejecting Monique.

"I don't know what Tyrone's doing with her, I really don't."

"Well, I hinted at that one day when he was complaining about her being jealous and he made it obvious what he's doing with her!"

"What do you mean?" she asked in a way that made me wonder for a moment why she was so interested.

"Well, when I asked him why he didn't leave her, he just said *'A man's gotta do what a man's gotta do.'* And then he burst out laughing.

"Dirty bastard! Typical man, always led by his dick!" she laughed. "And what about you and your plans? Are you any further forward with sorting out Tyrone's financial situation?"

She was a good friend and she knew all about us waiting on the sale of the painting and about our financial set-up so I didn't mind her asking in the least.

"Well, the painting's going up for sale in London in two months or so and there's a lot of interest in it. Once it's sold then it'll take about another month before he'll be able to access the funds. But we're taking advice on how to proceed because obviously he doesn't want the Government here or in Britain helping themselves to a lump sum in taxes."

"And what will you do then?"

"Well, the idea is that I'll go back to England."

"Do I sense a *'but'* coming here?"

"I'm not sure... I'm happier here than I ever thought I'd be. I can't bear the thought of leaving Eliza."

"But you wouldn't be leaving for ever, would you? You could come back whenever you wanted to see her."

"I know."

"Or you could always stay here indefinitely. Would you like to do that?"

"No, well... I'm not sure. I mean, I am enjoying being here with Eliza but I know that I need to get back home soon, there are things I can only do in London. And besides, there are things about London that I miss, the shops, the theatre... just the busyness of it all."

"So life in paradise isn't all it's cracked up to be, then?"

"Not for me to be here permanently. It's not like I'm on holiday, you know, staying in a luxury hotel or villa with a pool. I take Eliza to the beach a couple of times a week and that's it. It's well different from a holiday and as much as I love it, it's an island, a small island and I need to get off! But then again, I just can't imagine life without seeing Eliza." I didn't say that it would also be difficult to imagine life without Tyrone, too, and that I hated the thought of leaving him, jealous of whom he might be with or even find love with that wasn't me.

"But you could spend part of the year here and part in London. That way you'd get the best of both worlds."

"Perhaps. I just haven't really got my head around things yet, it'll be easier to think once Tyrone's got his money and can start to put his plans for the two of them into action."

"I hope his plans don't involve any long-term commitment to Monique," Megan said. "I mean, you wouldn't want her as Eliza's step-mother, would you?"

"No! I bloody well wouldn't. She's already got two other kids. One lives with his father on Barbuda and her mother takes care of the other one. I'm sure she'd like nothing more than to set up home with Tyrone, especially once she realises he really is rich."

"When he's rich he'll have the pick of the women, so why would he want to stick with miserable Monique?" Megan chuckled. "He'll be spoilt for choice. Women for miles around will be beating a path to his door!"

"Don't tell him that, it'll send him off the rails," I said, making light and trying to bury the anguish her words had caused me, as we turned off the main road and took the back way to Jolly Harbour. In spite of her comments, it felt really good to have my friend back in Antigua again.

Chapter Thirteen

We threw ourselves into the Carnival spirit. Although Megan didn't like the beauty pageants and the calypso contests either, we still went along to lots of the events that were being organised every night. The atmosphere was always electric and wherever we were – Dickinson Bay, St John's, English or Jolly Harbour – our nights seemed to involve a lot of drinking rum punch and dancing. We'd both roll home together either to Potters, where she'd top and tail with me in my bed after we'd crept past Tyrone carrying our shoes and making exaggerated *"Ssshhhh!"* noises at each other, which inevitably woke him up, or to Jolly Harbour and then I'd have to leap out of bed early the next morning to get home to look after Eliza by seven thirty which was when Tyrone left for work.

A couple of times Megan came and had dinner with us and we sat talking until late, the three of us enjoying ourselves just like old times. Megan and I joined in J'ouvert Morning, which was a blast and like nothing I'd ever experienced before. The floats, which form a sort of procession, kicked off at 4am, so we didn't go to bed. We followed them around the streets, dancing to the deejays and drinking and enjoying ourselves until around half past eight when we were both shattered and so we bought ourselves a big Antiguan breakfast of salt fish from one of the dozens of food stalls that had sprung up, and sat on a wall to rest our feet and enjoy it. And then we made our way home.

Tyrone hadn't wanted to do J'ouvet Morning.

"I've done it a lot of times but it's new for you. You go ahead and enjoy yourself," he said, smiling selflessly. He'd been keen for me to go out and make the most of Carnival and seemed happy that I was with Megan. My suspicion that they may be interested in each other was obviously groundless as the only time they were in each other's company was when I was there. If I limed I was with Megan and when Tyrone went out to the pageants and the calypso he went with Monique. Everyone was happy!! And Megan, Tyrone, Eliza and I all went together to watch the Carnival parade on the final day. Monique didn't come with us because she was *'playing mas'* which is what taking part in the parade is called.

"Can't wait to see that!" Megan had whispered to me when she'd heard. "It'll be a sight you'd pay to erase from your memory!"

It was a wonderful, and in some ways quite surreal afternoon. One mas troupe after the other paraded through the town. We found a spot on Market Street in the shade to watch from. The procession was a huge, wonderful rainbow of colour and people and music. Nobody in the street could stand still; every single spectator, even the English tourists, were swaying and shuffling to the music. And then, a metallic, hammering beat started pounding through every cell of my body; throbbing, thumping, jumping. But this had nothing to do with the mother of all hangovers I was still suffering from; rather it was coming from the Hell's Gate Steel Orchestra, a 40-piece steel band packed onto the back of a float that was making its way down High St and swaying precariously through thirty-five degrees while actually leaving the ground with every clash. And behind them a magnificent mas troupe in purple and gold wiggled and strutted their stuff. Traditionally-built matrons in thongs and fishnets rippled and shook alongside trim, toned teens.

"You see some nasty things at Carnival sometimes," Tyrone said, shaking his head at the sight of some of them.

One such matron, pendulous breasts swinging and straining against her tasselled bra, shimmied towards us, threw her arms around me, said, "Hi, Honey!" and planted a sweaty kiss on my cheek. I thought that the heat, noise, rum and atmosphere must be causing me to hallucinate because under her glitter and makeup I thought I recognised one of our neighbours, Miss McDonald! Now most Sunday mornings while I drank my coffee, I'd sit on the veranda and watch the parade of elegant local ladies going off to church; a multi-coloured flock of exotic birds gliding down the road on their way to give thanks and praise to the Lord, all dressed so gracefully and stylishly I could be forgiven for thinking they might be going to a society wedding. And there among them I'd always see Miss McDonald, a lady of a certain age who runs the local ironmonger's store in her own, slightly prim, but always absolutely proper way. In her demure, navy blue silk suit with matching spotted blouse and standard-lamp hat, clutching her Bible to her bosom, she always wore a subdued, sombre, pious air. But not that afternoon!

With all the practice and erotic expertise of a pole dancer she 'wined up' against Tyrone who, of course, joined in with lots of whooping and as much enthusiasm as if she'd been a babe of eighteen. The two of them ground their bodies together and gyrated their hips, punctuating their dance with wild, sexy pelvic thrusts until with a saucy wink and a whack on his arse she disappeared back into the throng of dancers, purple feathers shaking and cellulite a-go-go. Tyrone needed a long swig on his beer to recover.

"She's some woman!" he said as we all laughed together.

But before we could get over the spectacle of Miss McDonald a buzz went round the crowd as the Prime Minister, Baldwin Spencer appeared with his mas troupe. Resplendent in red and black, carrying a feathered lance in one hand and a Wadadli Beer in the other, he jammed his way through the streets like any other Antiguan on this Carnival Parade Monday; simply having a ball. I grinned to myself for the rest of the afternoon as I imagined Miss McDonald the following morning, back in her shop at nine o'clock on the dot, elegantly coiffeured, demurely dressed, quietly spoken, counting out nails, nuts and bolts into brown paper bags as if her alter ego had never been unleashed. Tyrone saw me smiling.

"Enjoying yourself?" he asked, putting his arm round my shoulders.

"Great time!" I said, smiling back at him, trying to ignore the thrill I felt at his touch. I really needed to find another Chris soon! I was so ready for sex again. Anxious that he shouldn't pick up on my feelings, I pulled back from him and bent to look into the pushchair and smiled again at the sight of Eliza bouncing up and down and gurgling, shaking her head, eyes wide open, taking in all the sights.

"You can't say she's not Antiguan!" Tyrone said, leaning down and taking both her hands in his and dancing with her. She squealed and laughed and gave him the biggest smile in the world. Megan, who always had her camera at the ready and was a keen photographer, let off a few snaps and then showed them to us. They were just gorgeous; the love between the two of them, father and daughter, was almost tangible in the photo.

"I'll e-mail them to you," she said.

"Oh, yes please!"

"You stand there, too," she said to me. "Let me get a great shot of you all together. You can put it next to the one I took at Easter of the three of you in the yard."

Tyrone and I crouched forward, one either side of the pushchair and Megan got her photos. And right at that moment Monique swooped. She and another girl grabbed Tyrone and made a sandwich with him in the middle and Monique facing him, rubbing his head into her almost naked breasts and thrusting her hips against his crotch while her friend wined up behind him. They were in tiny turquoise bra tops and matching thongs and when your bum is the shape of Monique's that's some sight!

"The things you see when you haven't got a gun, as my old granny used to say," Megan said sending me into fits of laughter.

"I think I must be switched off at the mains," I said. "You know, I don't quite get all this thrusting business. I mean, if it wasn't Carnival it'd be sexual assault, surely? Is it because I'm white or European that I don't get it, do you think?"

"Trust me, it's not a black or white thing. There's women and girls playing mas today who are having a great time and enjoying themselves without having to strip naked and act lewd," Megan said. "But I never expected any less of her!" she added, sucking her teeth and tossing her head in Monique's direction. "You're right. Outside Carnival that would be sexual harassment!"

Tyrone finally managed to disentangle himself from the women, although he'd obviously had a very enjoyable couple of minutes. But we could see that the parade was nearly over. Once the last float passed us we meandered back through the streets, stopping to chat to people we knew, deciding to go to Redcliffe Quay for an ice-cream. By this time, worn out from having such a good time, Eliza had fallen asleep, so we ordered three ice-creams and sat down in the ice-cream parlour's little garden to eat them.

"I can't believe I've only got two more nights!" Megan wailed. "Why does vacation pass so fast when work goes on forever and ever?" she asked us.

"You coming back again soon?" Tyrone asked her.

"Not until Christmas probably. I haven't got any more vacation left, I've already used it all up, what with coming here at Easter and all."

"Still, it ain't over til it's over," Tyrone said. "You still got two more nights so what you got planned?"

"A quiet one tonight!" I said. "I can't go out tonight."

"What?" Tyrone looked shocked. "Your friend's only here for two more nights and you're gonna stay home tonight?"

"Why don't you come down by me and I'll cook us something and we can just chill on the terrace for a couple of hours? You can come, too, Tyrone, if you want. And bring Eliza," Megan offered.

"No, thanks. I've got work tomorrow. But there's no reason why you can't go, Vic."

"Okay! As long as it's not a late one, Megs. I know what you're like. How many times have we said we're having an early night and then it's been three o'clock?"

"But three o'clock is early!" Megan joked. "No, it won't be a late one, honestly, it won't. After all, you're not the only one that's been out all night for the last two nights."

"You two have fun together. You can talk girlie-talk and whatever else you talk about."

142

"And then tomorrow night – one last lime! And we will be out all night!" Megan said. "So if you've got plans, Tyrone, you'll have to cancel them! You're babysitting while Vic and me party!"

"What plans would I have?" he asked, looking dismayed and affronted.

Chapter Fourteen

Eliza had been fractious all day. She seemed to have the snuffles and I thought she probably had a cold coming on. I'd given her some Calpol and tried just about everything I could think of. She didn't want to watch TV, she didn't want to play, she didn't want me to take her for a walk in the pushchair, she didn't want food, she didn't want to go in the baby-walker and she didn't want to sleep in her cot. I'd tried them all and they had all resulted in her screaming and getting upset, and I couldn't bear to see her upset and crying. She was usually such a happy little girl that seeing her like this was distressing.

All she wanted was to sit on my lap and for me to cuddle her. So that's what I did. I'd been scheduled to have a Skype conference with Rhonda about another exhibition of Eleanor's work, some paintings that had never been seen before and had come to light in her studio after her death, but that had had to be cancelled. We could talk another time; Eliza was poorly and she needed me.

I made sure there was plenty of water in the cool-bag as we sat gently swaying in the hammock seat under the big flamboyant, which since Tyrone had put a fence around the house had become the garden's only tree. I could tell that Eliza was running a temperature and I kept fanning her to cool her down. Inside the house was hot, even with the fans going and I really thought it was better for her to get some fresh air in the shade, out of the sun. I'd decided that if the Calpol didn't work and she was no better tomorrow morning then I'd take her to the doctor's, but I was sure it was just a little cold. I looked down at her beautiful face, the closed eyes with their feather-fan lashes and a little bubble inflating and deflating from her nose as she breathed in and out. I reached for a tissue and gently wiped it away and leaned forward and kissed her on the forehead. I felt such a huge surge of love for her that tears sprang to my eyes. I couldn't love her more if she'd been my daughter instead of my half-sister. And I had to face it; I was going to miss her like hell when I went back to London. How could I not see her every day? How could I climb into bed at night without knowing she was okay and without giving her a goodnight kiss? Just the thought of that burst the dam of self-control and I found myself crying as I held her. Christ! What was wrong with me? I wasn't even due on so I didn't know why I was so weepy and emotional. But it felt like something was over; that our good times were coming to an end and something bad was coming. I shivered as if someone had walked over my grave. Megan was leaving tomorrow and it would only be a matter of weeks until Tyrone's money came through and he could start putting his plans into practice. I knew I had work to do in London and a life to get on with. But was that what I really wanted? The truth was that I didn't really know what I wanted. I felt restless and unsettled. I'd thought about organising myself so that I could spend part of the year in Antigua from now on and I knew it was feasible, although I hadn't said anything to Tyrone about it. I had enough money to buy a small holiday home or to stay in a hotel for a couple of months each time I came so I wouldn't be intruding into his life. But even so, that was in the distant future; the near future was the reality and that meant a good few months back in London to start with. I felt my eyes closing and dozed alongside Eliza in the shade, the slight swing of the hammock rocking us both.

She woke up a couple of times, crying out and violently shaking her head at everything I suggested. All she wanted was water, so I gave it to her with some Calpol in it and after ten minutes or so of crying and wriggling she settled back to sleep again on my lap. By the time Tyrone came home I was exhausted from doing nothing but swinging back and forth all day and trying to pacify Eliza.

"She's not well," I said as he came to join us on the swing and bent to kiss her. "Don't wake her up! All she's done when she's been awake today has cried herself back to sleep again. I'm not sure I should go out tonight."

"You crazy? It's Megan's last night. And besides, I'm here. It doesn't need two of us to look after her, does it?"

"No, but..."

"What can you do that I can't? You think I'm not capable of looking after my own child?"

"Of course I don't! It's just that she's fractious. Her little nose is snuffly."

"So, if she's uncomfortable I'll give her some medication and if she gets worse we'll go to the hospital."

"I don't think she needs the hospital, it's just a cold, but sometimes a cold can make you feel really rough. I've been giving her Calpol."

"Then that's what I'll do, too," he said, loosening his tie.

"Go and have your shower and then I'll get you some food."

He disappeared back inside the house to come out again ten minutes later wearing shorts and a vest and carrying a plate of salad and cold chicken I'd left in the fridge.

"I was going to make you something a bit more substantial," I said.

"No worries. This is fine." He dug into the food. "So, where are the two of you planning to go tonight?"

"Somewhere in Jolly probably. Dinner at Melini's then either up to Sugar Ridge for a drink or the Sports Bar. We'll see what happens from there on I expect and who we meet along the way."

"Are you staying at Megan's?"

"Probably."

"I think you should. You won't be able to have a drink if you're driving."

"I know. And to think I rarely used to touch alcohol," I said, laughing. "This island's turning me into an alcoholic!"

"Welome to Antigua!" he said laughing. He finished his chicken and salad and took the plate into the kitchen. "Here! I'll take her," he said, coming back out again. "You probably want to go and get ready, don't you?"

"It's only quarter past six. Megan's not expecting me until after eight so there's no rush."

I stood up and gently put Eliza into his arms as he swapped places with me and sat on the swing. I picked up my empty glass and went inside, taking it to the kitchen. I was thirsty and I opened the fridge to get a Diet Coke and was surprised to see two bottles of Chilean wine in there, a Sauvignon Blanc and a Shiraz Rose. To my knowledge Tyrone wasn't much of a wine drinker; he was more of a beer man.

"Are you planning on getting drunk while I'm out enjoying myself tonight?" I asked him as I opened my can of Coke and walked back to the veranda.

"What?"

"The wine in the fridge?"

"Oh, that! A guy came by the office selling it at a good price so I thought I'd get some."

"You don't usually drink wine."

"I know! But I thought you might like it. Who knows? If I have a glass I might get to like it, too. Help yourself if you want some."

"No, I'll stick to this, thanks," I said, waving the can at him. "I'll probably have enough tonight. I must say, I'll miss Megan when she's gone, but it'll certainly give my liver a holiday!"

He laughed and I went inside to have my shower.

I chose a pale pink halter-neck sundress that I knew suited me. I put on my usual make-up; loads of mascara and eye-liner and just a faint touch of lip gloss. As I brushed my hair in the mirror I was taken by surprise at how like Eleanor I was. I shouldn't have been as we'd always been alike, but for a moment it brought back memories of her with a jolt and a wave of sadness broke over me as I realised once more that I'd never see her again.

An hour and a half later I was ready to leave, although I suddenly didn't feel like partying. Thoughts of Eleanor had left me feeling sad. I gave myself a shake to lighten my mood. Eliza had woken up while I was in the shower, but she'd actually been in a really good girl for her Daddy. Honestly! He must have thought I was lying or exaggerating when I'd told him how she'd been for me through the day. She laughed and smiled at him even when he gave her a sponge bath.

"You can see her eyes are heavy; she's definitely sick. Aren't you, my little angel?" he said as he put fresh, clean pyjamas on her.

"Well, if she needs it the Calpol's in the bathroom cupboard. Give her one more spoonful before she goes to bed, that should be enough," I said. "And ring me on the mobile if you need me."

"I'm tired of telling you. Go out and enjoy yourself with Megan. I can look after Eliza. I won't be calling you at all."

"Night, night, my darling!" I said, leaning over and kissing her. "See you in the morning!"

Chapter Fifteen

When I got to Megan's I was beginning to feel more like partying but my mood changed again when I saw she was still in her shorts and bikini top and was already on the way to being pissed. Two friends of hers from Jolly Harbour, Lance and Cheryl had been there all afternoon, apparently. They were an English couple who had lived in Antigua for about twenty years and seemed to eke out an existence by doing any number of odd jobs on boats and in gardens and houses. He had his hair in long dreads, which I always think looks awful on white men, especially middle-aged ones as it makes them look grubby, and both of them had skin like leather from spending so long in the sun.

"They came five rum punches ago!" Megan said, screaming out laughing.

"And we'd better go," Lance said. "I know the two of you have plans for tonight and we're actually on our way to St John's."

I was pleased they were going. Not that I didn't like Lance and Cheryl but I didn't really have much in common with them and found them a bit heavy-going. And, besides, I didn't want them tagging along all night. They were a pair of professional free-loaders who never seemed to be without a drink in their hands, yet were never seen to put their hands in their pockets.

"Do you want one for the road?" Megan asked. "Go on! One for the road!"

They must have seen the look on my face because they declined and were out the door in two minutes flat.

"Go and have a shower and get changed and I'll clear up here," I said, picking up the dirty glasses, a bit annoyed with Megan for not being ready and messing up our plans. After all, we'd agreed half past eight, not quarter past nine. And I was hungry.

"Sorry! I know you're put out because I'm running late, but I'll be just five minutes," she said, disappearing up the stairs. I heard a thump as she reached the top.

"You okay?"

"Just slipped and knocked my shin. No problemo!" came the reply. I shook my head, but couldn't be angry with her. She was just being Megan and she'd been a great friend to me. I heard her bedroom door open and a couple of minutes later the shower came on. Suddenly, I realised that my eyes felt gritty and a headache had started. That was probably why I'd been a bit tetchy with Megan; I'd probably caught Eliza's cold. But then again, if I was honest, I felt a bit edgy because Megan was leaving. We'd had a great couple of weeks – and I'd had an amazing summer – and now it was all coming to an end and I was suffering from separation anxiety. I'd always hated goodbyes and just knew that I would be upset and tearful the following day when I left Megan's early in the morning. I gave myself a mental shake. I mustn't start feeling sorry for myself! I sniffed. I hoped it wasn't a migraine starting. I didn't get them very often but when I did they came with a vengeance. I dived into my bag and found some aspirins. I went into the kitchen and helped myself to a glass and some water and I was just downing the aspirins when Megan came down the stairs, appearing to have sobered up and a vision of loveliness in a white and lemon linen maxi dress.

"What's wrong?" she asked, seeing me down the tablets.

"I think I've got a cold coming on. Eliza's been off-colour all day and now I think she might have passed it onto me."

"Poor you!" she said, hugging me. "Where do you fancy for dinner?"

"Well, it's your last night, so you get to choose," I said.

"Pizza! Let's go for a pizza here in Jolly and then we can get smashed locally. Not far to crawl home!"

I laughed, but by the time we got to the pizza place, my head was spinning and I knew that I'd be on the water and Diet Coke all night. Some last night party this was going to be!

Chapter Sixteen

I felt as if I was a real party-pooper. I tried hard to match Megan's mood, I really did, but she'd already had the head start with all the rum punches she'd had with Lance and Cheryl and the half glass of wine I had with our pizza did nothing for me.

"Come on! Drink up! It's my last night!"

"I don't feel like drinking tonight," I said, realising I sounded lame and that I was really spoiling the mood.

"A toast to meeting up again soon!" Megan said, pouring wine into an empty glass and thrusting it in my hand. "To friendship!"

"To friendship!" I echoed, clinking my glass against hers and then taking a tiny sip. We'd shared a plate of prawns as a starter and then the waitress brought our pizzas. I'd ordered my usual Hawaiian and Megan a Seafood Special. I couldn't swallow it, though, as my throat had become so sore. Even the smallest piece of pizza felt as dry as a sheet of cardboard and so I left most of it. My head was throbbing and all I wanted to do was to go home to bed. Megan, surprised that I didn't want any ice-cream, called for the bill saying we'd move onto Sugar Ridge for some more cocktails. I couldn't think of anything I wanted to do less but couldn't abandon her at eleven o'clock on her last night in Antigua. But then just as we'd left the restaurant and were about to get into the car I heard someone calling our names. I turned and saw it was Bobbi, a singer-songwriter I'd met at the Open Mic sessions and had introduced to Megan a couple of nights earlier when we were out in St John's. She looked her usual glamorous self, and she was with a very handsome, younger man, who she introduced as her brother Jude. I saw

Megan's eyes light up with lust and approval as she allowed him to kiss her hand.

"We're just going to Sugar Ridge for a drink. It's Megan's last night," I told them. "Why don't you join us?"

They readily agreed and I was pleased that they did. Now I could have just one drink and then go home without feeling I was leaving Megan in the lurch or spoiling her fun. Staying out all night drinking was the last thing I felt like now. I just wanted to get home. It looked as if she could have all the fun she wanted with Jude, who couldn't take his eyes off her. And when we got to Sugar Ridge I was happy to see that there were other friends there who she could enjoy herself with. Maddie, a Canadian who'd made Antigua her home and who ran a fishing charter company was sitting at the bar with Delia and Stefan, two Swedes who owned a villa in Jolly Harbour and who divided their time between their two homes and Chester, a local guy who owned a catamaran and worked with people off the cruise ships, was sitting at a table talking to three American girls. Everyone called out to us and waved as we took a table in the far corner. It was a very warm night, but even so, I was sweating profusely. I knew that I was running a temperature and so decided to have just one drink and then whatever happened, I was going home. I needed water, aspirins and rest. And so, fifteen minutes later I patted Megan's arm to get her attention. She and Jude had been deep in conversation ever since we'd arrived and Bobbi was talking to one of the barmen. A bell rang deep in my muddled brain; I'd heard something about her having a boyfriend who worked at Sugar Ridge. So, given that I was Ms Wallflower, nobody was going to notice if I left.

"Oh, honey! Don't go!" Megan said when I finally got her attention. "Have another drink!"

"Megan, I feel really lousy. I have to go now because if my headache gets any worse I won't be able to drive. I think it might be a migraine and you know how bad I get them."

"But you're going to stay at mine!"

"I was, but I just want to get home to my own bed. Really. And then I'll ring you in the morning to talk about what time I'm picking you up for the airport."

"Have I abandoned you tonight?" she asked, standing up and throwing her arms around me. "Is that why you want to go home?"

"Of course not! Don't be daft! I really do feel like shit. And you have a great evening!" I said, nodding my head in Jude's direction. "You can tell me all about it tomorrow," I added and we both giggled.

"If you're ill tomorrow don't worry about the ride to the airport. I'll get a taxi and come by yours to say goodbye."

"Okay. But I'm sure I'll feel better after a good night's sleep," I said, giving her another hug. Then I waved goodbye to everyone else and got back into the car, counting the seconds until I could climb into bed, put the fan on and sleep until tomorrow. I drove back to Potters very slowly indeed; so slowly that I don't think I got out of second gear. My eyes hurt enough as it was and when the glare from the full beam of the idiot, oncoming drivers hit them, the stabbing pain was unbearable. And to add to it, I then had those coming up behind me with their full beam reflecting from the mirror straight into my eyes, flashing their lights because I wasn't driving fast enough for them. What is it with these people? The full beam

155

blinds you so if anyone or anything's in front of you you've got no chance of avoiding it. I cursed every driver who didn't dip their lights all the way back home. And just when I thought it couldn't get any worse, as I got through Jennings it started raining heavily, too. Twice I slammed the car down into pot holes that I hadn't seen, the second time almost biting off the tip of my tongue. I wondered if I really should have stayed in Jolly Harbour, but dismissed the idea instantly. Megan was set for a session and I knew I'd never have kept up. I just wanted my own bed

Chapter Seventeen

I ran through the rain from the car to the veranda and slipped my feet out of my high-heeled sandals and left them by the door, Antiguan style, and then let myself into the house as quietly as I could. I was feeling really rough by this time and on top of that, I was exhausted from the stressful slow-drive home. Tyrone slept on the sofa-bed even on the nights that I was staying elsewhere which meant that I had to creep quietly past him. I didn't want to wake him up, or even worse, as he thought I was staying over at Megan's, for him to mistake me for a burglar and come at me with the baseball bat he always kept for our protection behind the front door. The house was silent, which meant that Eliza was sleeping; a good thing. I gently pushed the door closed until I felt the lock click into place and then turned to pick my way silently across the living-room to my bedroom at the rear.

I'd taken about six steps and had drawn level with the sofa when I stubbed my toe against something hard and heard the distinct chink of glass. My eyes had become accustomed to the dark and there was a shaft of light from the nightlight in my bedroom shining through the open bedroom door and streaking across the floor. I bent to look at what I'd kicked and saw that it had been one of two empty wine bottles which were lying next to two empty wine glasses.

And next to them was a pair of white lace panties.

I snapped my head around and looked at the sofa and blinked hard at the tangle of black and white limbs lying on it. Tyrone was snoring gently with his head tipped back while a wild, tangled mass of blonde hair adorned his chest.

What the fuck was going on? What did he think he was playing at?

I was furious. We'd had an agreement; neither of us had ever brought anyone home. He'd never even brought Monique here. Or had he? A wave of doubt washed over me. I'd never brought anyone here, but could I be sure that he hadn't? Who knows what he'd got up to on the nights I'd stayed out? My stomach gave a lurch and with it my brain clicked into gear and suddenly everything fell into place. No wonder he'd been so keen for Megan to come and visit! No wonder he'd been happy to stay home while I went out with her! No wonder he'd wanted me to stay over at hers! That way he knew the house was his so that he could bring this girl home! And who the hell was she? I peered at her, vaguely making out a turned up nose and wide lips below the mane of hair. But from what I could see, she wasn't anyone I knew.

How dare he? How fucking dare he?

He was supposed to have been looking after Eliza, my darling little baby. How was she? Where was she? Had he taken her to his sister's for a few hours? Surely not! He knew she hadn't been feeling well. Stupid, irrational thoughts tumbled into my mind.

I rushed into the bedroom, not caring about making a noise now. I just wanted to see Eliza and to know that she was okay. Fuck him! Fuck the dumb blonde he'd brought home! Fuck the pair of them!

Two minutes later I let out a scream that came from the very depth of my soul and that was loud enough to wake the whole neighbourhood.

"Tyrone! Tyrone! Help! Call an ambulance! Eliza's not breathing!"

Chapter Eighteen

"I was looking after her," Tyrone said, his head in his hands. "I'd done what you said. I gave her the medication."

"But how much did you give her? Eh?"

"What do you mean? What you insinuating?"

"Well, perhaps your mind wasn't on the job, Tyrone. Perhaps your mind was somewhere else, with someone else."

"Don't be stupid! I looked after her. I did. I gave her her milk. I sat and held her for the longest time. I gave her the Calpol before I put her down for the night just like you said."

"Or perhaps you gave her an extra little spoonful to make sure she went off to sleep and didn't disturb you."

"I didn't do that!" he stared at me long and hard. "How can you even think that, Vic?"

"Well, what am I supposed to think? You tell me to go off and have a good time and before I'm even halfway to Jolly Harbour you're fucking some whore in our living-room." He hadn't heard me use bad language that often and my choice of words now made him wince, which I liked. Good!

"She's not a whore, Vic. It wasn't like that," he said quietly.

"Wasn't it? Well, that's what it looked like to me. You encourage me to go out, to stay out, to spend the night at Megan's. And why would you do that?"

"Because I wanted you to have a good time!"

"Oh, really? Do you think I'm stupid? Eh?"

He didn't reply so I steamed on.

"You're a liar! Are you trying to tell me it wasn't because you wanted to be sure the way would be clear for you to bring a woman home?"

His head shook from side to side and then he lowered his chin to his chest.

"It wasn't like that! For fuck's sake! You make it sound like I abandoned Eliza."

"And didn't you?"

"No!"

"Let me remind you of something, Tyrone. You wanted Eliza. You wanted a child. You wanted the chance to show the world that you could be a good father. You had something to prove. But you know what? You haven't proved anything! Nothing at all!"

"I'm trying to be a good father!"

"Oh, and that's what a good father does, is it? Eh? He brings home some tart that he's met and gets her drunk and gives her a good shagging while his little girl's lying ill in the next room. Is that what he does?"

"No!" He put his hands over his ears in a pathetic attempt to block out my words. "I'm doing the best I can. That little girl wants for nothing, does she?"

"She wants for nothing materially, but perhaps having a father with a sense of responsibility and decency would count more, don't you think?"

"I am decent and responsible! Christ! It was one night!"

"And let me remind you of something else. You wanted my mother to have your child; you put so much pressure on her that she died through giving birth to her..."

"Vic! That's not fucking fair! I didn't know she was dying, did I? You didn't know she was dying, no one did! Don't bring all that up again! Eleanor made her own decisions, so don't try and lay all that on me. Not tonight."

"The point I'm making is, that if you wanted a child so much you should at least be prepared to make some sort of sacrifice to look after her, especially after the sacrifice that Eleanor made."

"I have been making sacrifices!"

"Oh, really? Like what? What sacrifices have you made? Because from where I'm standing it looks to me like you're having the best of all worlds. I'm your free-of-charge live-in babysitter! I'm the one who's made sacrifices! I'm the one who's changed her life beyond recognition!" I paused for a beat to let my words sink in before I launched another tirade at him. "I've put my whole life on hold to help you with Eliza. I've left my comfortable life in London to come and live in some... some... shack with a selfish bastard who only thinks of himself! Me! Me! I'm the one that's done that!"

A nurse came out of a room at the far end of the corridor and hurried towards us before he had chance to react to my insults.

"Can I ask you to keep the noise down, please? I know you're upset and distressed, but we're doing all we can here. You're not helping anyone by shouting and arguing and you're disturbing other people."

"Oh, sorry..." We both looked at her, ashamed of ourselves.

"Perhaps you'd like to wait outside, get some air?" she suggested. "We'll call you as soon as we have some news."

"I ain't going nowhere! That's my baby in there!" Tyrone said. "And why is it taking so long? Is she gonna be alright?"

"She's suffered some sort of seizure we think and she's had breathing difficulties because her nose is blocked with the cold. But as I've said, we're doing all we can and the doctor will talk to you once she's stable and we know what the situation is. Really, he will. We'll find you as soon as we have some news or she when she stabilises."

"Thank you. Sorry. We'll be quiet but we'll wait here," I said and she turned and walked quickly away to get back to our sick little baby. But once the nurse had gone Tyrone proved the insults had hit their mark and that he had by no means finished with me.

"So you're just gonna throw that all up in my face now!" he said in a stage whisper. "That's what you really think of me and my home? I didn't twist your arm to stay here and look after her for a while, you offered!"

"Tyrone, be fair! I was left with a tiny, premature baby that wasn't mine. I took care of her as best I could until I was able to bring her here to you. Then I agreed to stay on and help you look after her until you got the money from the painting. I know that and I accept it. But I'm not Eliza's mother. I'm not even her full sister, I'm a half-sister. And I think that for a half-sister I do more than my fair share of looking after her, don't you? I look after her all day every day..."

"That's because I'm at work! And I take care of her every night. Every single friggin' night!"

"Because you're her father and that's what father's do!"

"But I need to have some sort of life, Vic!"

"And so do I!"

"But you're always out. It's me that's home alone most nights."

"Yes, and that's called RESPONSIBILITY," I found myself raising my voice at him again, losing my temper. "If you've got a daughter you've got to look after her. You have to put your own needs to one side for a time. Stop being so selfish!"

"Wanting a woman's company now and again is selfish?"

"Do you see me bringing any men back to the house? Eh? Do you? How many men have you caught me on the sofa with?"

He gave me a strange look and then turned away, sucking his teeth as he did so. But I wouldn't, just couldn't, shut up. I really wanted to hurt him so badly for what he'd done and the only way I could do that was with my words. I didn't just look like Eleanor physically; I surprised myself to realise that when I hurt, I had her sharp tongue, too.

"You haven't changed a bit, have you? You're still the selfish, beach-bum you were when Eleanor met you. Out for what you can get, pimping off women. I'm surprised at this one, though. She's a bit young for you, isn't she? I mean she probably isn't a day over twenty-five, but she must be giving you something. Oh, but wait!" My tone was taking sarcastic to another level. "You don't need the rich old ones now, do you? After all, in a short while you're going to be rich yourself. And meanwhile, me, the idiot here, is paying all the bills and picking up the tabs."

"Shut up! Shut up!" He stood inches from me; right in my face. "Stop being such a fucking bitch! How can you say all that to me? Is that what you really think? Is it?"

I took a step back, realising that I'd provoked him to the point of losing it completely.

"All the time you're being nice to my face, smiling and acting happy and yet you really think that I'm some kinda freeloading ponce. And I can't believe you're resenting paying for stuff when it was you who offered in the first place?"

I didn't answer him. I eased myself down onto one of the chairs and looked away.

"You're going on about this unspoken agreement of not bringing people home, but we also agreed about money. You offered to pay the bills until my money comes through! *'A fund,'* you said. *'An Eliza Fund'*. You offered! But don't worry cos I'll pay you back every fucking cent that you've spent on me, on my kid and on my house. Every fucking cent!"

"Well, you can talk! Don't accuse me of being two-faced when you've done the same! You pretended you wanted me to have a good time and enjoy myself when all you really wanted was to know that I wasn't going to be home all night so that the way was clear for you to bring her home. Is that being nice? Is that being honest? "

"It wasn't like that!"

"Oh, please! Give me a break! Of course it was like that! And how many other times has this happened?" I asked, thinking about my evenings in English Harbour and at the Open Mic sessions. "How many other times have I gone out thinking you're at home on your own with Eliza, not knowing that the minute my back's turned you've had company? Eh?

"None! I swear! This time was different. I was in a difficult situation..."

"You looked like you were in a perfectly comfortable situation to me!" Tyrone gave me a steely look and then he shrugged, full of bravado.

"Really, this is none of your business, Vic!"

"What? My baby sister is in there fighting for her little life because you didn't look after her properly," I pointed to the door of the Resuscitation Unit, "and you're telling me it's none of my business?"

Tyrone leaned back against the wall, visibly deflating before my eyes, let out a huge sob and covered his face with his hands, which I could see were trembling. A tear started to weave its way down his face and he brushed it aside and turned to look at me.

"Okay! Okay! I'll tell you what happened," he said nodding at a row of chairs to show we should sit down, taking the seat beside me in the empty corridor. "I met Lorna a while back, two years ago when I was first working on the beach. She was staying at the Mango Tree and well, you know how it is. And before you bring it up again, no, she's not old and no, she's not rich. Because in spite of what you and Eleanor thought and accused me of I didn't spend my time just looking for older foreign women to leech off. Although she didn't believe me and nor did you, Eleanor was a one-off. Yes, I spent most of my time on the beach; yes my income was from supplying weed to tourists but that didn't make me a bad person or a pimp!" He spat the word at me. "It was a case of supply and demand, you know that. And the day I met Eleanor she did all the running."

"Oh, yes! It's easy for you to slag her off and blame her now she's not here anymore!" I interrupted.

"Vic, I'm just telling it like it is. I was sitting with two young couples on the beach and Eleanor was a little way up from us. They was asking me things and I knew we was building up to a sale and that's what happened. As I stood up and said goodbye to them she called me over and asked me to put some lotion on her back. I started chatting. *'Sweet Lady'*, was playing on my ipod and so I started singing along to her, calling her *'Sweet Lady'*, playing up my Caribbean side, you know, giving it all the accent and the charm and she was lovin' it. She was! It was a bit of fun; we was having a laugh together. And then, before I knew it I was back in the villa with her. And the rest, well, you know..."

"So where does Lorna fit in?" I said, totally unable to keep my voice neutral.

"Like I said, I'd met her on the beach. Before Eleanor, long before Eleanor. And I liked her. She was cute, reminded me of a girl I'd known back in Rainham when I was at school. We went out for the rest of her stay and then she came back to the Mango Tree again, a month or so before I met Eleanor. And then before I knew it, she'd made surprise plans to come back to Antigua yet again to see me. But when she got here she couldn't find me because I was in England with you two. And then a couple of months ago she found me when I started my page on Facebook. She gave me a right slagging off, called me everything for standing her up and not returning her calls.

I told her that I'd been off island when she came back and that things had been a little complicated for me lately. Then the next thing I know, she said she was coming back to see me and to spend Carnival here and I didn't know what to do."

"What do you mean; *you didn't know what to do*?" I said, mocking him. "You should have told her the truth, that you have a daughter and that you don't bring women back to the house."

"But I like her and I wanted to see her."

"You could have still seen her."

"How? How could I have seen her? When could I have seen her? On Saturday afternoons?"

"So when did you see her on her previous visits? I'm sure the Mango Tree doesn't allow beach boys in!"

"On her first trip I had the keys to a friend's flat in Bolans. He was away and he'd asked me to keep an eye on the place. And the second time we took a room in St John's a couple of times."

"Oh that was classy! Why couldn't you do that this time?"

"What was I supposed to do? Take Eliza along with me? Christ! I'm getting all this shit for taking her home, what would you do if you'd found out I'd taken Eliza with us to some cheap hotel?"

"But why lie to the girl? Why lie to me? If you'd told me you were going out one evening or two or three, even, I wouldn't have minded. I've stayed in when you've gone out with Monique. I'd have just thought it was her you were out with; doing something with her, for Carnival or staying over at hers. You manage to see her, don't you? How many times have I looked after Eliza in the evening or at the weekend so you can go and get your rocks off with her? And what's her take on all this with Lorna by the way?"

"Well, obviously, she doesn't know."

"Obviously!"

"Look! I'm trying to tell you the truth here, okay? So give me a break, woman! It's easy now for you to say what I should and shouldn't have done and how you would have agreed to this and that, innit, but I think you'd have caused a fuss and been cussing me off just like you are now."

He stopped for breath and I just looked at him, shaking my throbbing head in disgust with what he'd said to me. But seeing that I wasn't going to argue the point he carried on.

"And, well... when Megan got in touch and said she was coming for Carnival it seemed like that would be the answer to the problem."

"Oh, I see! Push me out with Megan, pretending you wanted me to enjoy myself and have a good time while it was all so that the coast was clear for you and ... her." Then something occurred to me. "Tonight's not the first time she's been to our place, is it?"

He sighed at being caught out and then shook his head. At least he had the grace to lower it.

"No. She's been round every time you've been out with Megan. I couldn't get away to her, so it just seemed easier for her to come by us. That way I could explain all about Eliza and what had happened and she could see her for herself."

"And I'd guess she was alright about it, then? I mean, given that she's come back every night for more?"

"She doesn't know the whole story." He was suddenly uncharacteristically sheepish.

"What? What do you mean?"

"Well, she thinks that you're Eliza's mommy."

My chin nearly hit the floor. What was he playing at? Who did he think he was?

"You've got a nerve! What did you tell her that for?"

He shrugged, lowering his gaze, unable to meet my eye.

"It just seemed, well, it seemed the easiest thing to do..."

"You bastard! Easiest thing for who?"

"Let me explain! I wanted her to come by us so that she'd see Eliza and then I could tell her the whole story. But when she walked in the first thing she saw was that photo on the wall of the three of us that Megan took at Easter, you, me and Eliza. She jumped to the conclusion that you were Eliza's mommy and then it was easier to go along with it rather than have to explain that your mommy was Eliza's mommy, too. I mean, even running through it in my head it sounded weird to me, and I'm part of it all, you know what I mean? Well, she got a bit upset and started saying she loved me and she thought I felt the same about her and it all got a bit heavy. So when I tried to explain what'd gone on... well... I told her that I'd been in Canada staying with some cousins and that I'd met you there."

"So, she thinks I'm Canadian?"

"Yes. She was upset enough, I didn't want her to know I'd been in England for three months and hadn't contacted her. I mean, it was lucky she didn't see any of the photos of me and Eleanor in the papers." He gave a huge sigh and shrugged his shoulders. "I know it sounds pathetic now, but I had to say something on the spur of the moment. It was easier to say I'd been in Canada and you were Canadian."

"You're unbelievable!" I said giving him a filthy look. If I'd be able to suck my teeth I'd have done so. "And so this Lorna, who thought we were a couple, had no qualms shagging you in our house while I was out? What kind of woman is she?"

He swallowed hard and closed his eyes for a moment before answering.

"She didn't know you were in Antigua. I told her that you were living in Canada."

"What?" I was appalled. "You can't help yourself, can you? You're such a liar!"

"It was the first thing I could think of. I couldn't tell her you were living with me. It sounded sort of suspicious. She'd never believe I was living in the house with you and nothing's going on with us. So I said you were in Canada."

"Well, she's knows I'm not by now! And if she'd stopped to do the sums she'd have realised that the dates didn't work out, or anything."

"Well, I sort of made it sound like we'd had a one-night stand as soon as I got there and we..."

"But surely she could see I'm living with you... in the house..."

"No she couldn't. I mean, you was never there and I hid your toiletries and stuff from the bathroom in the linen bin until she'd left and then I put them back before you got home, and she never went in the bedroom for nothing so she didn't see your clothes."

"And she's seen Eliza..."

He nodded.

"Eliza seemed to like her," he said, realising immediately that he'd put his foot in it again when he saw my face. The thought of her, that woman, holding, talking to, playing with my little Eliza made me feel sick with pain and jealousy.

I stared at him Tyrone disbelief and disgust. I couldn't believe he'd been so devious, so two-faced. All the time I'd been thinking he was being kind and considerate towards me, he was being totally selfish; it was just so that he could get away with having a good time. He'd simply wanted me out of the way so he could bring a woman home. And then something else occurred to me.

"Did Megan know what was going on?"

"Of course not!"

"Only... well... the two of you seemed sort of close. I mean, you knew she was coming for Carnival before I did."

"That's because we're friends, Vic. You can't think I've been with Megan, surely? Or that she knew about Lorna? I'd never have told her that..."

"No, of course you wouldn't!" I retorted, realising that there was no way Megan could have known. "She would have told me and dropped you right in the shit!"

"Megan's your friend and she's my friend now, too. And she'd run it by me before she booked her ticket just in case you'd had to go back to London or something and wouldn't be here. That's all it was; we wanted it to be a surprise for you. That is the truth. Honest."

"It's not been the only surprise."

He reached over and took my hand, squeezed it tight and turned to face me. I felt myself blush at his touch. His skin felt warm against mine.

"I'll make it up to you, Vic, I swear I will. You and Eliza. Just give me the chance to show you that I can be a good father; that I'm not a bad person. Please?"

I took my hand away and sat on it.

"Make it up to me? What? Will we go out for ice-cream? Or take a drive to the beach? How exactly do you make up for neglecting your child, Tyrone?"

"There's no talking to you, sometimes, Vic! What more do you want me to do? How many times do I have to say that I'm sorry?"

Chapter Nineteen

I didn't know how to answer him. He was right; my giving him a hard time wasn't going to undo the situation or make Eliza better. I felt so churned up, my head was splitting and I felt sick. I was beyond furious at what he'd done. So, as we sat in silence for a while I went back over the night's events in my mind. They ran like a surreal nightmare sequence in a film. In spite of everything, I could almost feel sorry for Lorna. When I'd rushed back into the living-room shouting and screaming, Tyrone was off the sofa in one fell swoop, brushing me aside and running into the bedroom. I was shrieking hysterically at him to do something; to call an ambulance.

"Get the car keys, we're going to Mount St John's," he said, "There's no time to wait for an ambulance."

Holding Eliza closely to him, he'd managed to pull a vest over his head and some long shorts over his bare bum with just one hand and then he'd slid his feet into flip flops and was out the door. Lorna had grabbed her dress and was holding it up to cover herself as she knelt on the sofa.

"What's happening? What's going on?" she asked in bewilderment, her Yorkshire accent strong. Well, of course I realised now why she was bewildered; she'd thought I was in Canada and had wanted nothing to do with Tyrone and Eliza.

Ignoring her completely, I ran out behind Tyrone and jumped into the driver's seat. Lorna was left alone in our house, naked, forgotten, unacknowledged and abandoned. I wondered if she was still there or if she'd simply got dressed and left. If she had the door would be unlocked. Why was I even thinking about an unlocked door at a time like this?

The drive to the hospital had taken five minutes maximum. Tyrone was in the back of the car with Eliza across his lap. All the way he was breathing into her mouth and massaging her chest in an attempt to stimulate her heart and revive her. I'd turned my head to look at them at one point.

"Keep your eyes on the road!" Tyrone had snapped at me between breaths.

He was out of the car before I'd even pulled to a halt and sprinted into the Emergency Unit with Eliza in his arms, bellowing for help, which had come instantly in the shape of two nurses and a doctor who'd disappeared into the Resuscitation Unit with our precious bundle. And then the waiting had begun.

"What the hell are they doing in there? Why is it taking so long?" Tyrone suddenly stood up and started to pace up and down.

"I don't care how long it takes as long as they make her better. That's all I want; for Eliza to be better so that we can take her home." I put my knuckles to my mouth in an attempt to ward off the physical sickness I was feeling; my stomach was churning and my guts were in knots.

"Yes, you're right." He came and sat down next to me again. "Shit! We've had our share of waiting in hospitals, innit?"

I glared at him and he seemed genuinely not to realise why.

"What do you mean *'we'*?" I asked him.

"Well, you know, with Eleanor in London and that."

"You don't know the half of it!" I retorted. "You spent half an hour one morning trying to persuade her not to have an abortion. You weren't there for the fall-out from that decision; I was! I was the one left picking up the pieces. I was the one who spent hours and hours waiting in hospitals with her. Waiting for appointments with gynaecologists, oncologists, obstetricians. And then sitting with her, holding her hand, watching her die. It was me! Me! Not you!"

"Oh, Christ, Vic! Please, please don't start all that again! How many times do I have to say I'm sorry for that? I don't know what more I can do." He shook his head. "And it's... it's hurtful to think that you're still harbouring all this resentment towards me. You know, I think we're friends, I think we're getting along well with each other. But all the time you still fucking hate me because of Eleanor."

"It's not that," I said. I wasn't going to say I didn't hate him. I wasn't going to make it that easy for him. I was hurt and angry and I was being a first class bitch but I couldn't help myself. "But after tonight's little episode, how can I even think about leaving Eliza with you? I'll be worried sick all the time I'm in London. I'll be waiting for the phone call that tells me about the next disaster. Waiting to hear of the next terrible thing that's happened to her because of your selfishness, because you've put yourself before her. And what's she going to have? Eh? A procession of step-mothers? Of different *aunties*? Of waking up every morning to one tourist after another in her daddy's bed?"

"For fuck's sake, Vic, stop it!" He threw himself onto his knees in front of me, grabbing both my hands in his. "Stop trying to make me feel like shit over tonight! Because, believe me, there's nothing you can do or say that will make me feel any worse than I do already. I'm not just beating myself up, I'm torturing myself. I'm slowly killing myself. If I had a knife right now I'd stab it in my own heart. I wouldn't need you to do it to me." Tears were running down his cheeks. "I know I fucked up tonight. I fucked up big time. Big time! And I'd give anything to turn the clock back a few hours. But I can't."

"Oh, so you admit it, then? You admit that if you'd thought a bit more about your daughter and a bit less about yourself, thought with your brain and not your dick, then we wouldn't be here."

"Stop it! I didn't ignore Eliza! I checked on her five or six times while you were out."

"You were snoring your head off when I came in!" I spat at him. "I even kicked your empty bottles and you didn't wake up! Remember the bottles? You know; the ones that someone just happened to come by your office selling?"

He lowered his head in what I hoped was shame and not just pique at being caught out in another lie.

"You'd had such a fucking good time with Lorna," I smiled smugly at my own weak pun, "you'd worn yourself out and you were sleeping it off! Poor little Eliza might have been screaming her head off and you'd never have heard her!"

"All right! I had a session with a woman! I admit that, Vic. I'm not denying that. I'm a young bloke, I'm not a fucking monk! But I didn't abandon or neglect Eliza. I was in the next room and I kept on checking on her. I did! On Mommy's life I did! I swear to you I did." He brushed his tears away with the back of his hand and sniffed. For a moment he looked childlike and vulnerable and I was tempted to hug him and tell him it was all going to be alright. But I didn't. He sniffed again.

"I'm entitled to some sort of life, Vic. I needed a woman. All right? I needed a woman. I like Lorna and she likes me. We were just having a little fun. But after tonight, I swear that's it. I've learned my lesson. When I'm looking after Eliza I'll give her my full attention and I won't bring no more women home. And besides, it's not as if I'm ready to settle down and play happy families with Lorna. She says she loves me and wants us to be together but honest, that's never gonna happen. She's jumped the gun. All the being in love's on her side not mine. We had a holiday fling that's all it was and she's come back and we've seen each other again. But now it's over." His eyes narrowed and his expression was really serious. "So don't you dare say how I'm gonna bring a load of tourists back to be a string of mommies for Eliza. Don't you dare say that!"

He was still kneeling before me and he grabbed my forearms and held them tightly. I struggled against him but he held on.

"You're hurting me!"

"And you're hurting me!" he said glaring into my face. "Can't you see how you're hurting me, for fuck's sake?"

"Good! You deserve everything I've said to you. And more!"

I glared at him and he held my gaze for a couple of beats before his shoulders slumped and he gave a little chuckle.

"You can't deny you're Eleanor's daughter." He lifted his hand and touched my hair. "Same golden hair, same large eyes. Same barbed tongue! But a different way of hurting me."

"Well, what do you expect? At the moment I could murder you."

"You're missing the point, Vic. That's not what I'm talking about." He looked straight at me and slid his hands from my forearms down over my wrists until he was clasping my hands, wrapping his fingers around mine. Without taking his eyes from my face he slowly raised my hands to his lips and kissed my knuckles. The tingles shot up my arms all over my body. "I'm talking about us. About you and me."

"Us? What 'us'?"

"The 'us' there could be if only we'd stop pussyfooting around each other and just be honest. The 'us' I want."

I stared at him, unsure of what to say and frightened that I might be getting it all wrong; that I was misinterpreting or misunderstanding what he was saying, hearing what I wanted to hear and giving his words a twist that he'd find either sickening or laughable. I gulped.

"You want honesty, Vic? Right! I'll be honest with you. Totally honest. I'm sick of all this living separately in the same house. All this pretending we're sister and brother. Cos we ain't."

"What... what are we then?"

"You tell me!"

We sat in silence, staring at each other for what seemed like an eternity but was probably less than a minute, during which time my feelings ran across the whole emotional spectrum and back. I was still unsure of what he was saying. Oh, I knew what I wanted all this to mean, but fear still held me back. So I waited for him to speak again. And he did, gently stroking my hands and caressing my arms with great tenderness as he spoke.

"Look, Vic... I know how I feel about you and I need you to know. And if it gets me a slap, so what?" he shrugged. He waited for me to answer but I couldn't trust myself to speak. And besides, I didn't know what to say. He squeezed my fingers with his thumbs and gave a wry little smile before he continued.

"I can't do the skirting around each other anymore, pretending I feel nothing for you. There are times when I don't know how I've kept my hands off you or how I haven't told you how I really feel about you. And I don't know how you haven't realised how I feel! And I can't do the pretending I'm having a good time when I'm with Monique or out with someone else, because I'm not having a good time. The only good time I ever have is when we're together; the only good time I want to have is with you. I want to cuddle up with you on the sofa at night to talk about how our days went, or simply hold each other while we watch TV, not sit on different chairs facing each other across the room. I want us to be like a normal, loving couple doing the things that normal, loving couples do instead of keeping our distance and going out with other people. I want to date you. I want to share my life with you. And my bed."

I felt myself go scarlet at what he was saying. I was still afraid I was missing something, that he'd suddenly shout 'Joke!'. But the scary part was that he seemed to be deadly serious.

"Look... I've had feelings for you for a long time, you know what I mean? A long time. Even when I was with Eleanor. From that morning by the pool when we drank Mommy's ginger beer. From that moment I saw you in a different light but I couldn't do nothing cos I was with Eleanor and you'd made it clear what you thought of me. And then when she told me about the baby things got well complicated, with the abortion that wasn't an abortion and... I loved the way you stuck up for me that day in the clinic. You didn't have to, but you did. You tried to see things from my point of view and I liked that. But when we left the clinic I was upset and I wanted to get back home. Maybe I should've stayed, but getting together with you wasn't on the cards then, was it?"

He paused and looked at me almost shyly, unsure of my reaction. I swallowed hard, but couldn't speak. So he carried on.

"And I know you have feelings for me, Vic, don't say you haven't! Good feelings, loving feelings. If not, what's all the fuss about tonight?"

"The fuss tonight is about you neglecting Eliza to be with a woman."

"Don't talk shit! It's more than that, innit? You're mad because you think I left her on her own, although I didn't. But you've carried on like a jealous woman tonight. Like a wife or girlfriend. And all that questioning me about Megan, as if you though I was seeing her and you didn't like it. You're jealous, and that's good, cos it means you feel something for me. If you'd come home and found out I'd got drunk with a couple of mates tonight you wouldn't have reacted like that. I'm right, innit?"

I waited a beat and then I nodded.

"Okay. I admit it. I'm mad at you but, yes, I'm madder because you were with a woman."

"So, does that mean you do feel something for me? You do love me?"

I looked at him; his handsome face with its beautiful eyes and big open smile and its honest, childlike expression and was finally prepared to admit to him what I'd know for a long, long time: that it was impossible for me not to love him. I nodded my head slowly. A huge smile spread across his face and he put his arms around me and held me to him, kissing my hair.

"I couldn't believe it the day you came back... when I opened the door and saw you standing there... You was the last person I expected yet I was so happy to see you. I thought you'd come to see me cos you liked me, or wanted to be with me. But, it's like you coming here to bring Eliza to me... was ... was it something that was meant to be? Was it Eleanor's way of getting us together?" he said, burying his face against me.

I burst out laughing. It was nervous laughter to cover my own feelings, but I couldn't believe that he was being serious. He looked up, hurt.

"You are joking? Eleanor would have hated the idea of you and me getting together," I said. "You were the man who helped her relive her youth; who made her feel attractive, sexy and young again. All that hanging on you and kissing you in front of me, that was her way of making sure that I knew you were hers and so did everyone else. She couldn't have handled seeing you with me. It would have really hurt her." He thought about that for a moment.

"She might've hated it... But you wouldn't hate it?"

I stared at him and then slowly shook my head, realizing just what it had cost him to bare his soul like that and that I had to be honest with him in return.

"I wouldn't hate it at all."

We stared at each other for a moment and then he slowly leaned in to kiss me, as if he was scared of a rebuff or that I'd pull away. But why would I pull away from something that I'd wanted and dreamed about for so long? As his lips brushed against mine I felt my body jump with elation and a desire so strong that to have denied it would have been stupid and futile. I'd already denied it for long enough. It was true what Tyrone said; I did want a relationship with him. I'd known as soon as I'd got back to Antigua; as soon as I'd seen him again. I had to be as honest with him now as he had been with me. We both gently pulled away and stared into each other's faces.

"I've loved you, been in love with you, that is, for a long time. You know, that morning with the ginger beer you accused me of being jealous of you and Eleanor having sex while I wasn't getting any?"

"Oh, God! I'm sorry about that," he winced.

"No! You were half right about it. I was jealous, but I was jealous that it was Eleanor with you and not me. When she first brought you home I thought it was gross that the two of you were together. I thought you were a slob; a beach bum; a gigolo who was just out for what he could get from her and would then run off. Well, that was okay, I mean, I wanted you to run off. I didn't want you around her or us. But, then something changed. And you're right, it was that morning we shared the ginger beer."

He smiled and clicked his fingers.

"You see! I was right! I knew I was right!"

"Yes, but we didn't know that was the day she'd gone into St John's to have the scan that showed she had cancer," I said sadly. "Or that she would soon be pregnant. That was the same day that I started to see you differently and to realize that I was falling in love with you. Well, in lust at that point. And when it all went wrong in

London, when she told me she was pregnant and then you wanted her to have the baby, I was so upset and gutted I didn't know what to think or do. I was trying to support Eleanor, but the thought that you wanted to accept your responsibility to the child made me love you even more yet hate you at the same time for making my mother pregnant. You know?"

He smiled and nodded his head, encouraging me to go on, liking what he was hearing.

"I'd got you wrong on so many levels, although at the same time, the fact that it was a child you'd fathered with my mother that you wanted to keep was... well... like a knife being driven right through me. I was gutted when you left for so many different, complicated reasons. Gutted and depressed. Yet, there was really only one simple reason; I didn't want you to go because I was in love with you and seeing you, having you around, even if you were with my mother was easier, better, than never seeing you again. On the way to Gatwick I don't know how I didn't beg you to stay, but I felt sure you'd laugh at me. I never ever thought I'd see you again, let alone be living alongside you for the past few months and sharing your house. Although, I've been on the outskirts, haven't I? I've not really been a part of your life."

He sucked his teeth again.

"Course you've been part of my life, innit? How can you say that?"

I shrugged.

"Well, whatever, you're part of it now. You're all of it now. You and Eliza, of course. From now on we're a couple; we're a family. We're together the three of us."

"But it's not that simple is it?"

"I love you, Vic. I really and truly love you. And you've just said you love me. So what could be simpler than that? And besides, when we're together, with Eliza, it just feels right. Know what I'm saying? We're comfortable with each other. We've got to know each other gradually in difficult, strange circumstances and it already feels like we're a family. We're a ready-made family."

"But, you're forgetting something. Or someone," I said.

He looked at me strangely; genuinely puzzled at what I'd just said.

"Eleanor." I said. "Eleanor will always be a presence we can't ignore. You've just said I'm like her and I don't need you to tell me that, I can see it every time I look in the mirror. I'll always be thinking that I'm just an Eleanor substitute for you. When you're with me will you be thinking of her? She's gone so am I just the younger version that you're wheeling out."

"Oh, for fuck's sake! "

"No, Tyrone! Hear me out! How can I ever be sure that it's me, Vic, that you want and love for myself and not as Eleanor Mark Two? Will you be with me when you really wanted to be with her?"

"But I never loved Eleanor! She was a laugh, right? I'd never met anyone like her. She gave me a great few months, treated me like a king and we enjoyed ourselves together. But that's all it was. She was right when she said that. It wasn't some great love affair. All that stuff about wanting to get married was me just trying to put pressure on her to keep the baby. Don't get me wrong, I liked her. I really liked her. Who couldn't? But when someone's died it's easy to get..." he paused, seeking the word he needed. "Well, I suppose it's easy to get over sentimental about someone. She was a great woman, classy and fun to be with, but I didn't love her. But I am in love with you, Vic. I love you. How many times do you want me to say it? I. Love. You."

"But... isn't it sort of strange? Kinky even? You made love to my mother and now you want to make love to me? I feel sort of uncomfortable with that."

"Why?"

"Oh, come on, Tyrone, you can see it's not exactly normal."

"Nothing about this whole scene's normal, Vic! Okay, I made love to your mum. So what? She was someone I met, just like Lorna and Monique and a whole load of women before I met you. Your life didn't start the day you met me; you've had other guys. The fact she was your mum's got nothing to do with it."

"It's strange, though."

"It's only strange if you let it be. You look like your mum; you've got the same eyes, the same lips, the same body shape, the same hair. So you're my type, the type that I like. But I know you're a different person. You're your own person, not an Eleanor clone. You're a beautiful woman but you're good and kind and sweet as well. I love everything about you. You're a woman I've fought to keep my hands off for the whole summer and one that I've fallen in love with. I can't be more honest than that, Vic. And if that ain't good enough for you then we can forget this conversation and just carry on as we have been and say goodbye when you go back to London and then we both lose out on a once-in-a-lifetime chance of happiness. Not just for us, but for Eliza."

"But what will people say?" I cringed as I said it. I could hear Eleanor's voice scathingly saying *"Never care what people say about you, Victoria. Their opinion is none of your business."*

He gave a little snort of derision at that, shaking his head at my naivety.

"But half the village thing we're together already."

"What?"

"Sure thing! They see two young people living in the same house and they assume we're together. It's natural that they do."

"So why didn't you tell them we're not together?" I asked, uncomfortable to think they people had been talking about us. "Why didn't you deny it?"

"What? You want people to think I'm gay or something?"

I had to laugh at that. But there was another cloud hovering, ready to rain on our new-found happiness.

"And what about Monique? Where does she fit in all this?"

"She don't! She don't fit in."

"But you can't just drop her like that!"

"What? You sticking up for Monique now? You never liked her before."

"That was then, when she was your girlfriend. All I'm saying is she's always suspected there was something going on between us and now she's not going to like it."

"She don't have to like it! We dated and now we're not dating anymore. People break up all the time. And we're breaking up

186

because I've found the love of my life! Living right under my own roof; right under my nose."

He leaned forward and kissed the tip of my nose and then pulled me to him again. I was still uneasy about Monique. I knew she could cause trouble for us, but there was something else; something Fiona had once said to me shot into my mind. She'd been going through a bad patch with Daniel her man, who'd been staying out and not being able to account for his whereabouts. *"The trouble is that you can be with the nicest Antiguan, a really good man, but he'll always have a local girl somewhere on the scene who'll kiss his feet until he passes out."*

"It's just... will she still be around?"

"Of course she won't! I've just told you. She's history. Why would I want Monique if I've got you? You're enough for me. I'm a one-woman guy from now on. I promise."

"But promise me one other thing, if I agree to this madness, that is," I couldn't resist adding.

"Anything!"

"Drop the Caribbean Dude stuff! Just be yourself. And you don't have to be London Boy or anything else. Just you."

He burst out laughing at that, his eyes bright for the first time since I'd woken him up.

"But you might not like the real me! What then?"

"I already love the real you. So the choice is yours," I said, grinning back at him.

He leaned forward and kissed me again and this time my arms went up around his neck as I kissed him back and held him tight, tingling with excitement that soon, really soon, I'd be sharing love with this gorgeous, sexy man. The thought of that send a wave of pleasure crashing up my groin, leaving me feeling wet and wanting. His kisses moved from my lips to my neck and my ears and I'm sure that I started to groan with pleasure just as the doctor stepped out of the Emergency Room and started down the corridor towards us. We sprang to our feet, standing together, hand-in-hand, ready to hear the good news about our little Eliza; the third side of our family triangle; the gorgeous little girl that made our joy complete.

Chapter Twenty

I slipped the thin, dark dress over my head, pulled it down straight and smoothed out the creases that weren't really there in an automatic, nervous gesture, before sitting down on the chair in front of the mirror. I picked up the brush and pulled it through my hair, staring at my reflection as I did so. Eleanor's face looked back at me, my weight loss accentuating the likeness. I put the brush down and fastened my hair back in a large slide and then leaned back in the chair, closing my eyes and yet again, without any conscious bidding the memory of the first session of the superb, splendid sex that I was now sharing with Tyrone floated back into my mind in vivid, minute detail.

It had been rough to the point of being violent and brutal. We had gone for each other as soon as we got home from the hospital. The realization that we were in love, that we wanted each other with a passion, combined with all that had happened to us that night, meant we had both shared a primal need to connect with another human being in the most basic way; a reassurance and a reinforcement of life. Our senses heightened and aroused, we took each other, selfishly, sadistically and masochistically. Tyrone pulled me to him, pinioning my arms to the side of my body with his before the door had even closed behind us and started kissing me so hard I was biting my lips while kissing him back. Without letting go we shuffled through to the bedroom where he pulled my dress down over my breasts, ripping the thin straps as he did so and taking my panties at the same time until I stood naked before him. I pulled his shorts down as he took his vest over his head and we both reached out and roughly pulled the other to us; two bodies slamming against each other, tingling and trembling from the explosion and fallout of the other's touch. We found we were a perfect match; our bodies fated to fit together like pieces of a predestined jigsaw.

He gave me a hard push onto the bed, climbed on top of me and started to bite my neck, my shoulders and my breasts. He sucked on them so hard as if he wanted to drain my life's blood through them, while his tongue relentlessly beat my stiff, erect nipples back and forth in an increasingly frantic rhythm. Looking down and seeing his black face kissing my white breast, his ebony against my ivory, was such a sexy sight that I felt my clitoris contract and an electric shock jolt through my body. I pulled at his hair, holding onto it tightly, I scratched his back and that just spurred him on, biting my stomach and breasts while his hands slapped against my thighs. His head went down between my legs and I grabbed his braids, wrapping them so firmly around my hands in sheer ecstasy that I thought they would come off in my hands. His tongue slapped against me, harder and faster until I started to scream out my orgasm. And then he entered me with huge, hard, fast thrusts... five... six... seven... eight and then came his own primordial wail of pleasure before he collapsed onto me, shuddering, shaking and then finally sobbing *"I'm sorry, I'm sorry, forgive me!"* over and over again.

I held him until he was calm and his tears had subsided, this time showering his head and face with loving, tender kisses of delight and contentment, secure in the knowledge that he was finally mine.

The sound of Tyrone's cell phone ringing in the living-room jolted me out of my daydream and brought me back to the present, my stomach churning and bile rising in my throat at the thought of what the next few hours would bring. He didn't bother to answer it and I understood that. I forced myself to stand, brushed away the imaginary creases in my skirt again and braced myself at the thought of what lay before me in the next room. Yet I was still unable to prevent the tears that were already forming in my eyes that were so red and raw from all the crying I'd already done.

I shook my head and straightened my shoulders, took a deep breath and then I slowly walked into the living room where Eliza's tiny coffin lay.

Chapter Twenty-One

Tyrone stood next to the table that held the coffin, where he had stood since we had brought her home from the undertaker's; a sentinel refusing to abandon his post as if he was still trying to prove to the world his attention and devotion to her. He had broken with tradition in bringing her here, this but it was what he, what we both wanted.

"She's got to be here, Vic, at home with us, not in some funeral home. Not for her last night. Here, where she belongs."

I'd nodded in agreement.

"And then I'm carrying her to the church in my arms," he'd continued. "I don't want no one else touching her."

I went and stood next to him and put my arms around him and laid my head against his chest, staring at the white box, still unable to accept that my darling little sister was dead.

"You must go and change, Tyrone. Time's getting on," I said as gently as I could. We had both spoken in whispers since Eliza had been back in the house, just as we used to when she was sleeping in her cot or between us on the sofa and we had been afraid of waking her. Now we both would have given anything to be able to wake her. He didn't seem to have heard me. I reached up and placed a gentle kiss on his haggard, handsome face that bore the evidence of just how he had been ravaged by pain and grief. Neither of us had been able to eat more than the odd mouthful since Eliza had died.

"Tyrone," I whispered again. "You've got to get your suit on. It's almost time for us to go." He still didn't move. "I'm here. I'm with her. She won't be alone while you get ready. I'll be here." I kissed his cheek again and he slowly turned towards me and planted a kiss on my forehead.

"I'll be right back," he said, slowly breaking away from my embrace and going into the bedroom where his black suit and tie and white shirt hung from the wardrobe door. He did have to get ready, but I had my own reasons for wanting to be alone with Eliza, with my baby for the very last time. I took a step nearer and the perfume from the bright, beautiful spray of multi-coloured tropical flowers which covered the length of the coffin, wafted up and enveloped me. I reached out and touched them, my fingers caressing the deep green velvety leaves then lowering to touch the cool wood beneath them. I leaned forward, the waterfall of my tears dropping through the foliage, collecting in little pools before slipping over the edge and onto the table top.

What I had to say was for Eliza's tiny ears only.

"Oh, Eliza, it wasn't supposed to be like this; this wasn't in the plan. It should have been the three of us, all together. All living happily ever after. All together, here, in our own little paradise. You've got to believe me, Eliza, I never meant to hurt you, not you! You were the one who brought us together; you were the reason I was able to live alongside him, close to him and be with him. You were such a huge part of our lives and we couldn't... still can't... imagine a life without you in it. Oh, Eliza! I didn't mean it! It was a moment of madness..." I gulped and let the tears fall unchecked now onto the coffin that held her.

"I only put the pillow over your face for a moment... I just wanted to shock him... to make him realise what he was doing, how he was hurting us both and destroying what we had and what we could have. All together. The three of us. A perfect little family. When I came home and saw him sleeping with that naked girl... saw her wrapped in his arms instead of me... I just saw red. It should have been me he made love to... not her but me! It was me that spent all my time looking after you and instead of wanting me and being with me, he was with someone else. With a tourist! In that moment, Eliza, I hated him and I wanted to punish him. Yes, it was him I wanted to punish. Not you! I was tired and I felt ill and I wasn't thinking straight. And so I did it. I just wanted to scare him, to make him see what he'd done. I thought you'd just cough or cry out, and he'd come running into you. I never thought you'd stop breathing like that or I wouldn't have done it. Honestly! Of course I wouldn't have done it! Why didn't I just stop to think that your little nose was blocked? But, how was I to know that on top of the cold you had a virus that was weakening your heart and the strain of trying to breath made it stop and that nobody, not Tyrone, not the doctors, nobody would be able to rouse you or get that tiny little heart beating again? How was I to know, my darling? I never ever wanted to hurt you. You must believe me, Eliza! You must believe me..."

I lay my head on the coffin, trying to get close to her. I was hyperventilating, my breath coming in a series of syncopated sobs. My life had run out of control. I was out of control. I was insane; I had to be to have done that to Eliza. Being in love had made me do something that was beyond crazy. I took a deep breath and started speaking to her again.

"I have to tell myself that you're safe with Eleanor now; safe with Mum. I have to believe that. I do believe it. You're sitting on her lap, holding her hand and listening to her tell you the most wonderful stories, just like she used to with me. She'll cuddle you to her, wrap you up in her sweet, perfumed embrace and you'll be safe and secure and happy forever."

I felt calmer thinking that; thinking about Eliza and Eleanor together. Eleanor had been Eliza's mum, not me. And now she'd be taking care of her little girl again. It was a comforting thought. And there was still one other thing I wanted Eliza to know before she left me... left us.

"I'm going to try to be happy ever after, too, Eliza. Isn't that good? Although today I feel as if I'm never going to be happy ever again. You see, guilt is a dreadful thing. It's the worst emotion of all because you just can't shake it off and it eats away at you. And for the rest of his life Tyrone will think that he was responsible for your death. He'll believe that it was all down to him. Oh, don't get me wrong! I won't ever throw it up in his face. I haven't blamed him at all. In fact, I'll never mention it to him again. Why would I when there's no need? But because he feels so guilty he'll always be trying to make things right with me. He'll never leave me and he'll never look at another woman, because for the rest of our lives he'll be trying to make up for the way he behaved on the night you died. This handsome, sexy man that I've adored and wanted for such a long time is finally mine and he'll always be mine. But I have the biggest guilty secret buried deep inside my heart. You and me, we both know the truth about what happened that night. But I'm not saying anything. I'll live with the guilt and not pay it any attention or let it eat away at me. I'll tell myself what the doctors said over and over again, that you died of a virus, until, as they say, a lie becomes the truth. I know that Tyrone will always feel responsible for your death; but I will have to do my best to forget that the one who really killed you was me!"

I heard the bedroom door open behind me and Tyrone's footsteps crossing the floor. I leaned down and kissed the coffin, my crying becoming a howling as the time to say goodbye to her for the very last time drew nearer. I felt his hand caress my shoulders and slowly I stood up and turned into him, my tears soaking his jacket. His hand brushed my hair away from my face and I raised my eyes to look up at him, still strikingly handsome, his pained, gaunt expression enhanced by his suit and tie. He looked like he belonged on the pages of an upmarket men's magazine. Our lips brushed briefly, then he put on his shades, took a deep breath, turned and in one swift, strong movement lifted up the coffin and slowly walked outside with it to where all our friends and neighbours were waiting; to walk the longest half mile of our lives from our little house to the local church where we would have to say goodbye to our own, special, sweet little lady.